PROOF

OF

EXISTENCE

PROOF OF EXISTENCE

A NOVEL

DANIEL VERGARA

YORK AVENUE PUBLISHING

Published in the United States by
York Avenue Publishing.

Printed in the United States of America.

Cover design by Daniel Vergara
Page design by Eric Lopez

First Edition

CHAPTER ONE:

CLARISSA

1954

"I don't really feel like they see me." "You don't?" "Not really. It's like there's so much there, but I'm always afraid to step in and disrupt it." "Disrupt the cycle or..." "Disrupt the changes. There can be big changes here and there." "Okay, let's go back a bit." "Sure." "They appear to you..." "Yes, that's right."

"When they appear...and I know you say they have different faces, but do they speak directly to what you're experiencing or is it an experience within itself?" "Oh, completely an experience all on its own, Doctor." "Hmm. And do they speak to you directly? At any time, or do they just...occupy? If that makes sense?"

"Sometimes it's really hard for me to go to sleep without taking the pills you've prescribed, Doctor." "It pleases me to know that the Thalomid is helpful." "It certainly is. I don't have the spells I used to have and I'm able to have a rest before my husband comes home." "I'm glad to hear it but let's not veer off Clarissa."

"Oh, I'm sorry Doctor, I get distracted." "It's quite alright. Glad to know the pills are working. So, back to the story at hand: how many of them come to you? In your dreams?" "Well let's see...so many." "At a time?" "No, not really. Sometimes they're alone and they speak...to themselves and to others. It really can be exhausting. Sometimes I just want to wake up from my sleep and..."

"Allow me to ask you this, Clarissa...do you speak to yourself when you're lucid?" "I...I guess so. Sometimes, when I'm glancing at myself in the mirror. But I suppose everyone does Doctor." "I mean, do you talk to yourself in the sense that you are 'someone else?'"

"Someone else? I don't follow." "Do you ever feel like these 'women' pass into you at any moment when you're awake? Become you for a while, speak for you, dress you up, that sort of thing?"

"Oh, dear. I don't know. I'm not quite sure. I don't believe so Doctor. Gee, is that even a possibility? That sounds absolutely ghastly!" "Don't worry Clarissa that's why we're talking about it here, safely." "Oh. Well, I don't really think I'm out of sorts when I'm awake, other than the sleep deprivation and the bothersome anxiety. But nothing too wild, I suppose."

"That's good to hear. I just want to know if perhaps you may need sufficient treatment. I don't want you to simply rely on Thalomid if there is more to this story. It can be all quite alarming for others to understand, so I need to know if those 'women' show up, so to speak." "Hmm. I'm second guessing myself now, aren't I?"

Clarissa lit up a cigarette and took a deep puff. "You don't happen to have an ashtray around, do you Doctor?" Dr. Schigerr looked at Clarissa tentatively and opened his desk drawer. He placed the glass ashtray beside her and said, "I don't remember you picking up this habit. Were you always a smoker?" "Oh dear, no. I don't think so. But it certainly relieves the pressure of being here."

"Pressure? Tell me about that. You never mentioned you felt any pressure. Pressure being here or pressured to be here?" Clarissa shrugged her shoulders flippantly, taking another slow drag of her cigarette. "Both, I suppose. It can be quite harrowing to drive up-town every week to meet with you in this damp cold weather. I'm not a fan of winters or moving in it. Every part of it exhausts me to no end."

"Well, I drive up here everyday, so I can sympathize. Clarissa, if I may, I'd like to be frank. Would that be alright?" "Please do Doctor!" Clarissa sat up, doe-eyed, brushing the ashes from her olive plaid skirt. She folded one leg over the other, perking her head up like a pied-winged swallow. "Have you ever heard of Schizophrenia?" Clarissa's eyebrows darted up, as she began to put out her cigarette.

"Oh, I most certainly have! Are you implying..." "Now, hold your horses missy. I'm not here to imply. That's not my job. I'm mere-ly asking you a question." Clarissa shrugged. "I have, yes...and?" "Well, have you heard of MPD? Multiple Personality Disorder?" Clarissa looked down, pensive, trying to connect the dots. "I believe that I might have, I'm not sure. Why?"

"Well," Dr. Schigerr began, grabbing his notebook and pulling his chair close to Clarissa. "MPD can occur when one's self has inter-actions with other people, within one's self. Or a person that takes on more than one character. Does that make sense to you?" "More than one character?" She asked. "Yes! I'll give you several examples: a lady such as yourself, can go shopping on a fine day, picking up fruits and vegetables or whatever sort of thing you ladies buy."

"Roast, maybe? Some detergent?" "Exactly. Right! And suddenly Clarissa, you can become someone else...a 'Piper?' A brassy secre-tary that likes martinis or a lady of the night..." "Oh dear, I'm no lady of the night! I don't know any Piper! Maybe you need to sit back over there, Dr. Schigerr!" Clarissa folded her arms, her mood changing and unsettled.

3

"You're not quite following me Clarissa. I'm saying that perhaps these 'women' from your dreams are not just in your dreams but types of people you're acting out?" "Acting out? What kind of acting out?" "Do you recall we spoke a few weeks ago about your child-hood and its volatile episodes of trauma when your father went off to war."

"I believe so, yes." "You said that all you could dream of were air-planes flying around, shooting at each other and that your father nose-dived into the sea. Do you remember that?" "I do. I'm aware of that conversation. Are we going back to that?" Clarissa's patience was beginning to run out. "I'm only saying that many of your child-hood traumas, as sad as they were, could have positioned you to be..."

"Prone to hallucinations and spooks? Like becoming these 'wom-en' to cope with the loss of my father?" "Yes! Yes my dear! Now we're on to something!" "So..." Clarissa added, pulling out anoth-er cigarette. Dr. Schigerr nudges the ashtray closer to her but she stands up and walks towards the window. She lights up the ciga-rette and indulgently takes a puff.

"You're saying that all of the 'women' in my dreams are simply a figment of my imagination and that they might be showing up for the world to see because I was a scared little girl?" She put one hand on her hip and blew out the blue smoke. "Not in quite that way, but yes." Clarissa held her cigarette up between her two porcelain fingers and stood there contemplating until the curtain caught fire.

Dr. Schigerr sprang up, ran to the wet bar across the room and threw a glass of water at it. "Clarissa please! You mustn't smoke near these curtains, they are exorbitantly expensive!" With her shoulders pressing back, Clarissa made her way to her chair and extinguished the cigarette. "So I'm bonkers, huh?" She asked, fidgeting with her ash blonde hair and fumbling for her pocket mirror.

"Not bonkers. Just in need of some help. But no worries. After a few sessions and some occupational therapies, I'm sure you'll be back on track." Dr. Schigerr scrawled across his pad and pointed at the clock. "Well, our time is up. But wow! How productive today has been Clarissa!

We've finally put a stamp on the real issues and there is nowhere else to go but up!" "I see, Doctor. Except, I don't have this...disease you're talking about." "Not a disease, a disorder." "Whatever it is, I don't have it, and I certainly don't want it! I know my husband wants me whisked away to the asylum in Barkersville but he's got another thing coming." Clarissa's soft and shy demeanor turned into a staunch resistance. "I'm not crazy. I don't have MPD. I'm not unhinged or crying out for help, Doctor. I'm having strange dreams, but that's all. If that's your professional diagnosis, we're done here."

"Clarissa, I understand your concerns. These are some strange and trying times as many doctors are all too eager to do off with their patients when they are diagnosed. It's plausible that you would react this way. But I'm not any of those doctors. It's a modern world and we're going to do all we can to get you back to normal. No hospitals for you."

Dr. Schigerr, wiping the sweat forming across the back of his neck, wrote a prescription. "There are some exciting treatments available soon, but for now, we'll continue with Thalomid and perhaps hypnosis next session. I do hope you come back, Clarissa. I find you to be an incredibly intelligent and thought-provoking individual who can overcome her obstacles."

Clarissa stormed off to her car, making her way towards the market. The images of fruits and vegetables as she made her way past the produce section made her stomach turn. She looked up at The Butcher and pointed towards the roast beef. "I'll also have some of the drumsticks. Thank you Charlie." "Of course Mrs. White. Anything else?" "A few pounds of that luncheon meat and that'll be all."

Clarissa's heart was racing. She nervously opened the Pharmacy doors and quickly headed towards the magazine area. She picked up a copy of Mademoiselle and pretended to read the article about headstrong housewives. The Pharmacy was fairly empty and she decided to quickly pace towards the counter.

"Mrs. Phillip White." She practically whispered. "Phillip White? Okay, just a second." The young lady rummaged through the back section and then picked up the phone. "Hughes Drug Store? How may I help you? Uh huh? Uh huh?" She put her finger up, acknowledging Clarissa and continued to rummage through the metal bin.

"Clarissa?" She asked. Clarissa nodded. "...I'll do just that! Thank you! Have a good day!" She placed the bag in front of Clarissa and smiled. Clarissa placed the money on the counter, grabbed her bag and made her way out. "Clarissa White, is that you?" Clarissa almost fell over. She quickly grabbed a bag of mints and waved madly towards the young woman approaching her.

"Margaret!" "Maude! It's Maude darling, and in the flesh." "Maude how are you?" "I'm better, running into you. What are you doing way up here with us upper-crust folks?" "I was visiting my mother and thought I'd run some errands while I was at it." "Modern gal, huh? Your earrings are so pretty. Marvelous color! Always so put together, aren't you?"

"Thank you Maude...I must be on my way." "You stopped in to buy some mints?" She barked sarcastically. "That, and picking up some medicine for my mother." "Oh, poor thing. She must have a cold. I hate colds. And it's so damp out there, huh?"

"Yes it is." "I'm surprised you can walk through the snow with those heels and haven't caught your death!" "I have a car. I really must be going Maude. It was really nice to run into you again." "How's Phillip? Still working at that firm?" "He sure is!" Clarissa brashly placed her hand on Maude's arm, signaling she was done with the conversation. "I hate to be rude, but I really must be going. I don't want to get into traffic."

"I thought your mother was nearby?" "With all due respect Maude, that's none of your business." "Oh! My! I didn't realize I was intruding. I thought I'd strike up some interesting conversation since we're in the same area, at the same time and all. Silly me! I don't want to be such a nuisance."

"You're not a nuisance and I'm not trying to be rude, I just really have to get going. I've really got to get that roast in the oven before Phillip gets home." Maude smirked. "A housewife's job is never done!" Clarissa chucked the mints back on the shelf and left the store. When she got in the car, she placed the bag in the glove compartment and closed her eyes. Turning on the car, she began to hyperventilate. "Fucking...fuck...fuck...fuck...fuck..." She said, banging on her steering wheel.

Suddenly, there was a loud tap on her window and startled, she screamed. Rolling down her window, she realized it was the young lady from the pharmacy, handing her a prescription bag similar to hers. "Mrs. White? I'm sorry to startle you. THIS is your bag. I was distracted by the phone calls. We're so busy on Tuesdays, I sincerely apologize!" Clarissa grabbed the bag, waving and thanking her.

The young woman was standing there and Clarissa realized she needed the other prescription bag back. She opened her glove compartment and handed it to the young lady. "Thank you Mrs. White. Please be careful on the road! And have a swell day!" Clarissa drove off, uptown disappearing behind her like a puff of smoke. She spruced up her face and applied some lipstick.

Pulling into the driveway, she was met with the maid, helping her with all the bags. "You go inside Mrs. White, I'll handle all of this." "Okay, thank you Riva." Clarissa stood in her kitchen, perplexed by the weight of her day, removed her gloves and sat a pill on her tongue.

"Riva, do you mind if I rest my eyes here for a moment? I was thinking of making dinner but I can't possibly with all the strain I've put on myself today, you understand? Is it possible if you could stay longer and prepare it instead? There are some recipes right behind here..." As she searched for the right card, she toppled over.

"Ouch!" Riva grabbed Clarissa and helped her onto the sofa. "Are you alright Mrs. White?" "I'm fine...ouch...I'm okay. I think I twisted my ankle, is all. No need to worry!" Riva began to take off Clarissa's shoes and positioned her feet upwards.

"Don't trouble yourself Riva, thank you. I think I'll just lie here for a moment and collect myself." "Should I call Mr. White?" "Not at all, he's very busy today. Tuesdays are tricky for him. I'll be fine. Just some wrapped ice will do the trick!" "Right away Mrs. White."

Riva hurried into the kitchen, scooping out ice from the freezer. She placed a few on a small towel and made her way towards Clarissa. "Here you are..." Feeling something electric piercing her shoulder blade, Riva fell, knocking over a few picture frames, the ice spilling onto the floor. Clarissa, jolted up, putting her arm out. "Oh my God! Are you okay?" "Mrs. White, I'm fine." Riva got back up and placed the ice on the towel.

"I'll get some more, I was startled." "Startled?" "Yes, it happened again." "What happened again?" "No worries Mrs. White, I'm okay. It's been a long day." "No Riva come here. What did you mean?" "I don't want to say. Mr. White says that we shouldn't talk about these things and I want to respect that." "Don't do that Riva. What happened to you?"

Riva nervously placed the ice near her chest. "I just thought it was...electricity. Some static light of some sort. That's all." "Did it hurt you?" "I'm alright." "But did it hurt you Riva?" "Mrs. White, I'm afraid to say." "Why are you afraid to say?" Riva slowly handed the wrapped ice to Clarissa and exposed her right shoulder. Clarissa was at a loss for words.

"What in heaven's name?!" Riva's shoulder was bruised to a greenish blue and she pulled her blouse back over her shoulder. "It's nothing! It's nothing. We don't have to tell Mr. White." "What is that? Who did that...to you?" "Mrs. White, please don't worry yourself. It's nothing." "Stop saying it's nothing Riva! You have to tell me who's hurting you like this?" Clarissa caught a hold of her necklace and gulped. "Mr. White says..." "Did Mr. White do this to you?" Clarissa sat up, braving through her ankle pain. She looked at Riva in the eyes, holding both of Riva's hands in hers.

"Whatever you tell me, you can tell in good confidence. Not a word of this goes to Phillip, I promise!" Riva looked away. "Mr. White didn't do this to me...it was YOU." "Me? I did no such thing!" "Please Mrs. White, let me just start on supper and let's forget about this whole conversation." "What do you mean, 'me?'" "Mrs. White we do this every week. And I'm just not in the mood for it. So please, may I just start dinner so I can be on my way?"

Clarissa brought her knee towards her chest and slid her ankle across some sofa pillows. She held the melting ice to it and gazed at Riva until her eyelids grew heavy. They grew heavier until she fell asleep.

CHAPTER TWO:

JACINDA

I could feel my life spirit away into the mountains, clawing away from its mortal skin in the gloaming display of blood and teeth. I could hear the thunder roaring into my ears and the rain seeping through the soil and grit. I smelled the pits of circling roots dancing around my decaying skin as if it were someone else's dream. I did not shudder. I did not breathe. Another victim; another woman lost to the exploitation of this phallic world.

I didn't even know if I could love someone as much as I loved him. I was never allowed to know. He took that away from me. Shackled tightly to my innocence, I closed my eyes, though darkness already made its home in me. My ribs ached consciously for air, crushed into the fruit of the ground like a womb nestling its needy fetus. The erogenous onset of culpability began to trace over my heart lines; the mechanical glove of iron fists heeding.

And as seasons glorified themselves onto the vibrant vineyards, producing the ambrosia to wet the lips of cultured humans, I could feel my heart swim laps to the top, seeking an unreachable white gray shore. I felt him standing there like a martian, year after year wanting more from me. His blonde mane blowing in the wind, troubled with the blue regrets of yesteryear. His car rumbled profusely; two children in the backseat, and there I laid thin like a mosquito trapped in amber.

The wispy snow danced over me, the levity of time a clever reminder of my compounded life. Everyone was rapidly changing but I remained the same. As easily as taking part in an Accordo, fingers tightened along the partnering strings. He knew what made what sound. Crushing my head with a hammer.

I was now the lateral appendage of death's stem. I started to believe suddenly, like a ruminant over sparse land. I believed in my own elusive spirit, what weight I had in this and what I was capable of. I didn't have the luxury of another life. I had the here and now, wherever that was. But how could I forget? I was HERE and it was NOW.

Like a deep chiseled out cave where no crystal or rock was the same in its formation, I summoned my life force, intent on remembering every digestion, every rumbling. My internal workings flummoxed at my return. A literal body of work engulfed in her feminine prowess; discontinued and now in reproduction. I lifted myself, past the punctures and pain, a long conversation of design within my skeletal remains to resurface.

He never said, "I never meant to hurt you." I once had compassion for the cowardice even after. I had plenty of time to feel shame and pity. I felt shame and pity for myself, for him, for everyone he's ever hurt and loved. I could haunt him for the rest of his century if he lived long enough with that padded guilt. His reformation splintered under lock and key.

That rogue and nefarious heart beating like a German clock. I could design my ways to be bewildered and maddening, like a jaded lover blossoming into fright. It was a strange moment to think about. "Before I leave you alone, I need to tell you that you make me sad." He said, playing with my mind. His final words like hard candy cracking incisors intentionally. The audacity of his honesty rippled through a timeline.

And here I stood, in my complete framework, practically visible to the naked eye; deciding last minute that I wanted to be extant. Histopathology awakened, for men to take advantage of, as they always do. In my return, I did not wish to be a menacing force or offensive to my half life. For the imagination was now a process and not a prayer. The intent became survival.

I never liked the smell of tuna when I opened my lunchbox, and the children would circle me, pull my hair, kick at my feet and say "You stink! You're disgusting!" The teacher with her pinned up hair, book in hand, scowling from a distance, never the savior, always the voyeur. The pale desks lined up to one another, the blackboard at an angled distance, pencils being shaven away at their worn surfaces. Laughter and subtle bickering. I languished from being forced to endure that place.

And as I grew older, boys never minded my long legs and buckling knees; my beauty startled them into fits. They fought one another over who would smell my hair. Silly moments and intimate encounters of tag and I was always it, running tree to tree and car to car. Oh, how I enjoyed the sky, vacant of the sun but still harnessing her warmth.

Cold Octobers with patterned wool sweaters and cups of hot chocolate were remiss when my father sat at the head of the table scolding us into the walls. We knelt on rice and we whispered to each other how much we hated it here but we didn't want to leave.

I blossomed, as my mother said, when she secretly read my diaries and confronted me at my most vulnerable moments. I stomped my feet and rolled my eyes and the dog would hide under the table because her tone threatened the wallpaper in the hallway to flake and peel. But I suppose she meant well, though at the time it was like lightning striking the same tree twice, maybe three or four times.

Why was it that her cupcakes and cherry pies and her hugs and small talks were never as memorable as her incendiary moments where she'd break a plate or howl at my father for not having enough money to feed us. I remember he'd park his car outside the local supermarket to see if anyone needed a ride.

I'd immerse myself into Nancy Drew books while I sat passenger side; we'd go for three scoops of ice cream afterwards (mint chocolate chip, banana and fudge), but he never told me where he came from, where he'd gone or where he was going. His blunt sadness situated itself on our conscience.

At seventeen, I was at the corner movie theater with my friends watching Marathon Man or Logan's Run for the hundredth time. The theaters were still majestic but moldy and the ushers came out with their flashlights to make sure nobody was being fresh or had their hands where they shouldn't be. That was it. They didn't care if you snuck in or saw three movies back to back. They were more conservative than reactive.

When I learned I was pregnant, my mother had a fit, rushing me to her friend Ivy's house. "You were pious until the veil fell," my mother said, grabbing both my wrists and scolding me in front of three other women unabashedly. I felt more seen than ever. Visible and important even if I disappointed her. And I did. I disappointed her in a way that broke her heart. I never noticed my mother's eyes until they were swollen, red and melancholic.

"It's the Women's Movement Carol. You can't be so hard on her. We've all fallen into temptation before." Ivy pleaded, but my moth-

14

er was not swayed easily. She stood over me like the statue of liberty and placed her fingers on her pursed lips. "We have to get you an abortion. But they won't do it here, so we have to take a drive." The women surrounded her like a coven; they didn't question her authority and immediately I was storming away from town passing icy branches and plastic flamingo strip malls.

When it was over and four days passed, my mother sat at the foot of my bed, smacking my toes. She pressed her cheek to my knees and said, "I never thought I could fail so much until this happened. I never knew how bad it could get Jacinda. I wanted you to find a boy that could respect you until your wedding day. Someone who loved you enough to wait. It never occurred to me that it would never happen. And your father can't ever know or it would kill him."

She never saw me the same again. Instinctively, I wore an invisible Scarlet Letter. She timed my walks to the park and when I would get home. Her heavy-handed mistrust turned into manic episodes; waiting for me on the steps if I came home late from the library was her new normal. Though I was still young and inexperienced, for the first time, in her eyes, I was like rotten fruit being eaten by the vultures. It took time to regain her trust and it never came blindly and fully.

A few months later, my mother introduced me to a friend's son. He had a rugged country boy quality to him, full tussled golden hair and a smile that stayed put in my memory. He took his time with me, like a lion with his prey, pouncing when the moment was right. Each hour turned into days and pretty soon he had a promise ring around my finger. "I want you to go to church with me" he said, our time spent praising God and holding hands while sermons burned regret into my soul.

He needed to tame me to truly love me and that is what he set out to do. When my independence threatened his livelihood, he burdened me with jealousy and arguments. I didn't want to repeat the same patterns my parents had, but passion led us to that point. "God doesn't like it when you're at the Hamburger Alley with Scott and Meredith, you know."

He would wag his finger in my face and shame me for having friendships; his car appearing almost everywhere. In my mind, it felt protective and fiercely loyal and to my detriment, I almost made excuses for it. In fact, I did.

One morning, I sat in front of the mirror fixing my hair, thinking "Maybe he's in over his head with me. I'm too beautiful to stay put. I'm not his horse." At times, I'd lay on the floor listening to Minnie Riperton with my little sister Josie, running lines to her about life and Eddie and how he was becoming aggressive and foolish.
She dreamed up excuses for me to stay with him because he was "a gentleman" and "a christian" and "boys like that don't come along too often." She was living vicariously through me and I didn't want to disappoint her.

When Summer came, the temperatures threatened to scorch our skin and we made plans to go to the local pool. I laid out Josie, getting likely tans, and her red hair crisped up and that always made me chuckle. She'd splat sun tan lotion on my back and we'd gaze at every guy that glanced back at us. She wanted so badly to be noticed and I thought it was terribly endearing and desperate. But I also remembered being her age, so I threw her a bone and had them come over.

We had planned to leave the pool around 4pm to get ice cream, and then head home to watch "All About Eve." Around 3:30pm, Eddie pulled up in his Dodge Colt in tan cut off shorts and a gray tank top. He walked over to Dennis Seaver, sparking up conversation for a while, but I knew he was there for me. "Hey handsome!" Josie yelled, and splashed water on Eddie. He smiled and pointed at her and then bent down to return the favor. He glanced my way and blew me a kiss.

I loved when he blew me kisses. He had nice full lips and I loved to kiss them. Suddenly, all my doubts melted away and his hand was on my knees explaining work and how his mom was not getting off his case. He had been dealing with the death of his grandfather and felt pressured from his mother to go off to college in the fall. Eddie wanted to get a good job and move in with me. At least those were his plans.

I wanted to get back into the pool but Eddie asked me to walk him to his car for a second. "Okay, but only for a second Eddie. I don't wanna leave Josie alone for too long." "Yeah baby, it'll be two seconds. I wanna show you something." He kissed me and I obliged. My skin vibrated with redness, and the sweat dripped down my belly and onto my legs. It felt like the hottest day on earth. "What did you wanna show me hot stuff?"

He placed his arm around my waist and kissed me and I could feel how hard he was, pressed against my leg. "Oh no!" I joked. "Not now mister!" I laughed and he kissed me again. "Eddie, weren't you the one who wanted to wait?" "Wait?" "Yeah, wait." "Wait for what? To get married Jacinda? I doubt that's in any of your plans baby." "Why do you say that? Of course I'd love to marry you one day. Why are we having this conversation right now?"

"Cuz' my dick is hard and you want to have a heart to heart. But that wasn't the case according to Dennis Seaver." "Oh yeah?" "Yeah. He was telling me Josie and yourself were flirting all day with those inbreds from Callister Mills. You want that kind of life Jacinda Rose? To be forked behind the bleachers by those morons?" "I was just..." "You were just what Jacinda? Opening your legs to more men because immorality is your number one sin? When did you decide that I was nothing to you? Was it last month when you were out with Liz and Scott?"

"You mean Meredith?" "Whatever! You treat me like a dog, baby and I'm noticing that I'm just another boy toy for you. Is that it? Cuz' you can tell me now. I can take a hint baby. Just tell me to fuck off and I will." "I think you're overreacting and I'm just not in the mood to fight with you Eddie. Let's talk some other time." "Dismissing me like you always do.

Your momma is always making excuses for why you don't wanna pick up the phone. I'm always being canceled on...it makes me look pathetic Jacinda Rose! Don't you see that?" "Eddie I canceled on you last week because my mother fell down the steps and she hurt her knees real bad. It had nothing to do with you!"

"Sounds like a crock of shit, but okay I guess. I'm a damn good guy ya know...uh...Jacinda...I'm really good and I'm a catch and uh... whatever...don't wanna mess up your plans with your sissy. So, I'll just head back to my house and maybe I'll eat alone somewhere... whatever." "Baby, I'm sorry that you feel like I'm hurting you in any way.

I really am. Look at me! I'm sorry. I think you're an amazing guy. A real catch! You're such a sweetheart. But sometimes...you come off a bit strong. You know?" "I do?" "Yeah! Like showing up places unannounced and um..." "But I'm your boyfriend Jacinda Rose so I'm supposed to be everywhere you are."

"Yeah I know but...it starts to become...you know..." "Like what? Listen! I ain't no stalker so you can go ahead with that! That's for perves and rapists and I ain't any of those things, okay?" "I'm not saying you are." "You're sure as hell are insinuating it Jacinda Rose and I'm not in the mood." "Eddie baby, please listen to what I am saying to you..." "You better go back to your sissy before any of those Calister dicks try to finger her in the pool. You know they got a reputation for being like that...you know it!"

Eddie hung his head, scratching the tip of his chin. I stood there upset and confused, wondering if this was the beginning of something or the end of it. I wanted to hug him but I decided not to. He got into his car and drove off.

I walked back to the pool area and I gave Dennis a nasty stare, motioning for Josie to come on. "Eddie giving us a lift?" She asked. "Nah, he left. We kinda had a fight." "Oh no. I'm sorry. I'll get my stuff. Are we taking the bus?" Dennis walked over and tapped my shoulder.

"Hey Jacinda, I didn't say anything to Eddie. I promise." "Sure you didn't!" I responded, putting on my sunglasses. Josie and I walked out with our things and waited for the bus. "I have a few quarters Jacinda if you wanna call Eddie and smooth it out. I don't mind. I sure would love to have him give us a lift."

"I think we should just wait for the next bus. It'll be here in about half an hour. We can sing some Carly if you want. I don't particularly know any of her songs too well but you can teach me." "If you don't ring him, I will." Shaking my head, I walked over to the phone booth and after a few rings, his mother answered.

"Darlin' I do believe he's still at work. You want that number? Oh wait! He just walked in the door. 'Hey Snoo, your dolly is on the phone.' 'Don't say Snoo on the phone ma..geez...' 'Hello?'" "Hey. It's me." "I know it's you. What's up?" "So, I was wondering if you could give Josie and I a lift. I know you were just here but..."

"Okay! Yeah. Okay, I'll be there in a bit. At the pool right?" "At the bus stop near the gates?" "Okay, I'm heading over." "Hey Eddie?" "It's okay baby. Whatever it is…it's okay. I'll be there soon." "Okay. Thanks."

When Eddie arrived, Josie put her arms around him and said "You read the book I lent you? So good right? I'll need it back soon because I'm going to the library and I wanna pick out some more." "Don't you owe like 80 cents on some stuff there? They aren't gonna accept your library card kiddo!" "What do you know punk!" Eddie laughed and then put his arm on my shoulder. "Hey, you girls wanna get some ice cream?"

Around 6pm, Eddie dropped Josie off and asked me to stay behind to hang for a bit. I didn't want to make any more excuses because he was already upset, so I said yes. We drove for quite a bit with the radio on and his hand was in mine. It was really sweet how he kept looking over at me with lovebird eyes and it felt like he was being the bigger person and I appreciated that. "Where are we headed?" I asked. "You'll see." It seemed like we were off the path and he wasn't saying much.

I made small conversation but it wasn't reciprocated. It felt like he wanted to wait til' we got to our destination to really talk. Sex crossed my mind several times and maybe that's what he wanted to ease the day. I wasn't terribly opposed to it but I was still thinking about it. Maybe I was ready for it. Maybe not. I wasn't too sure. The main roads disappeared behind us and there were only tall trees and dirt. I ran my hands up and down my arms and said "This is gonna hurt tomorrow!" But he didn't respond.

"Oh? I've been here before. Isn't this that abandoned park no one goes to anymore? I hope there aren't any snakes or small animals, you know those freak me out." He patted my knee and smiled. He then parked the car and turned off the ignition.

There was a small awkward silence. Then he said "When I saw you at the pool, you looked so beautiful. I don't know if I told you that." "No, I don't think you did. But you're always so sweet so it's implied in your touch, baby."

"I know. I like to be affectionate with you." "Yeah." I had a lump in my throat. I was disoriented from the day and I was unsure of what was happening. I always felt safe with him, so there were no doubts in my mind...except today. But maybe I was afraid to confront the conversation we had a few hours back. How to approach it where he doesn't get upset again. "Jacinda, you are the ideal sweetheart. Any boy's dream, really." "Awe, thank you Eddie." "No really, I mean that Jacinda Rose, you're the IDEAL girl. I was proud to take you home to my mama. She really loved you."

"Well I really love her too. 'Loved me?' I don't follow." "Lemme talk for a second, cuz' I have to tell you something." "Oh! Sure. Go on ahead." "I get real nervous having these conversations and I sure hope you don't interrupt me while I do it cuz' I need to get this off my chest." "I won't." I felt him changing. "Thanks baby. Well, I like you a bunch that's already apparent.

And I met you, wanting to marry you off the back. Cuz' you're so sexy and beautiful and I don't think I've ever met a girl quite like you. That's the God honest truth Jacinda Rose. You are a beauty. More beautiful than I ever thought I could have. But for a while now, I've been noticing the feeling is not mutual."

"Well not really..." "Lemme finish please, I need to get this off my chest. I'm not gonna keep chasing after you. Like a dog. Like a damn dog salivating over some chops. My momma says I'm pretty smart

21

and I have self-worth and so, I just brought you here to tell you it's over and I'm done with you and that's the end of that. And don't try to change my mind."

He wiped his forehead and there was a silence in that unforgivable heat and it implied that now, he was allowing me to speak. To say something. And I did. "If you want to end this, I'm okay with it. I'm okay with how you feel but you have it all wrong. I never thought you were a dog, Eddie. Never in my entire life did that cross my mind. I just...want to be honest with you but I can't sometimes because boys don't like the truth and so I rather just leave it at that."

"So now I'm 'Boys?' I'm like everybody else out there? I ain't special to you? You comparing me to Dennis and Scott and those perves at the pool and the men that make you get abortions. That's my classification huh? Because 'Boys.' Wow. Predictable Jacinda Rose. You're just so fucking predictable dammit!" "You know what I mean Eddie! That girls like me aren't allowed to say 'Hey! I don't wanna date you anymore because I just don't love you like you love me.' I can't say that because you react like this...like an asshole!

And then, you wanna bring up my abortion like it's any of your business?! It is not!" "Well I didn't mean it in that way..." "Then how did you mean it?! Yes you FUCKING did! Because you think you own me and that's the problem! I'm tired of being seen like some pretty piece of ass. I'm a woman now! So if that fucking bothers you then GOOD! Go on your way and I'll go mine!" "Jacinda Rose, I didn't mean a word I said, I was just mad. I was just upset, that's all. I'm...I'm sorry honey. I just feel like no matter how my approach is, you won't ever want me. You just see me as some creep!"

"Eddie Sokoloff you take that back! I don't see you as a creep. I never have. I fell in love with you...for a while." "For a while?" "Yeah. A while. But you didn't let me breathe. I felt suffocated. Like

I was your property. Like I couldn't go anywhere or you'd be upset with me. Call me, leaving all kinds of messages to my mom, on the answering machine, my sister...following me! It's upsetting cuz' I just want you to be...normal...you know? Not like..."

"So you DO see me like I'm some creep! Okay, so then I'll show you 'creep.'" I'LL FUCKIN' SHOW YOU CREEP. He put his arm out, darting over my head as I slumped over, covering my face, thinking he was going to hit me. It happened so fast. The hammer was on his lap. He took it out of his toolbox a few days before and placed it in the backseat. I noticed it before, but I didn't think it was a big deal. Men carry around with their tools. No big deal. It was just sitting there. I slowly put my head up, my eyes fixed on that rusty hammer. "Say 'Creep' one more time." My nails were digging into my arms. My back was tense. "I said, say 'CREEP' one more time!'"

I was so scared, I could taste my tears. "I...never...called you... that...word." I muttered. "What word Jacinda Rose?" "I'm not gon-na say it." "SAY IT!" "No..." "Get out of the fucking car. You dis-gust me! Get the fuck out!" "What?" GET OUT OF THE CAR!" He screamed. "Eddie you're scaring me!" He reached over and I felt my heart almost come out of my chest. I couldn't move. He unlocked my door and with both his feet, he kicked me out of the car. I was on the ground and I was in a fetal position. I was shaking uncontrolla-bly. I wanted to run but instead, I began to vomit. I vomited the ice cream I had earlier.

He walked over to where I was and told me to stand up. But I couldn't. I was shaking from so much fear. He grabbed my arm and pulled me up. I could see his fist and the hammer in it. I felt the urine come down my legs and it was a terror you can't speak to anyone about.

"What a waste of time to love someone like you Jacinda Rose.

You've got spit up all over you. That's disgusting! What a fucking waste of my time. He said something muffled, from the side of his mouth but I couldn't hear a thing. Each blow changed me. When I opened my eyes, I was almost blinded by the blood coming down from my head. He attacked me like a wild animal, a trepidatious panic to bludgeon me to death. He spent the rest of that night digging a deep grave, tossing me over like a bag of autumn leaves. I laid there and laid there and laid there and laid there.

Until the ground shook with a raw intensity. The repeated patterns chalked across the cracked foundation. I was arriving to myself in whatever shape that it was. Like a furious river in motion, refusing to connect to oceans; independent and never ending its course. My mouth a dusky canyon, my hands the steep valleys, my feet the bedrock. I snaked into the bite like Medusa staring at her own reflection. I wondered, "Who was ready to turn to stone?"

CHAPTER THREE:

NIGHT TERRORS

"Here, have some coffee." Phillip placed the cup by her side. He disappeared into the bathroom, took a quick shower and came back downstairs. The cup was cold to the touch and Clarissa laid there with her hands folded behind her head. "What happened to your foot?" He asked lazily.

"It was nothing dear, just a sprain. The swelling is going down. How long was I out? What time is it?" "It's 9 o'clock." "9 o'clock?! Did you have dinner? Riva made pot roast. I could fix you a plate if you're hungry? Of course you're hungry. I'm famished!"

"There's no pot roast made, Clarissa. And besides, I had dinner with a few friends and I'm extremely tired. You can stay down here if you'd like." "No pot roast? But I bought some and Riva was..." "Yes, I noticed that. It made a wet hole in your paper bag. Next time, put it away before you decide to sleep off your entire afternoon."

"Sleep off my afternoon? I was at the doctor's today." "Oh yeah? How did that go?" "Well, if you have time, I can tell you." Phillip sat down and put Clarissa's feet on his lap. "You tell me and I'll massage your feet." "Swell. Just not too hard." "Sure thing. So how'd it go? Don't keep me in suspense."

"Well." "Well what? That's it?" "It went well. Yes. He asked me the usual suspect questions and prescribed me more medicine and said that I was just having headaches and that I should spend more time reading or picking up a hobby." "Reading or a hobby? That's his diagnosis?" "Well, he can't diagnose something that isn't there right?"

"I suppose. Maybe I'll give him a ring tomorrow and see what he says. He's not exactly looking out for my wallet's best interest." "It's so distasteful to talk about money like that. Don't concern yourself with those things. You have too much on your plate and you worry about me too much. I'm fine." "You're not fine dear. Things have been troubling you. Things...have been a bit...tense."

"Tense? That's a strong word." "It is? Well, I mean you've been out of sorts lately. Not exactly yourself. And we're all worried." "We?" "Well, yes We: Riva and I." "The same Riva that was supposed to make us pot roast but didn't?" "Riva is in New Mexico visiting her children. I told you that a few days ago. You took her to the airport?"

"That's right! Oh. I must've forgotten. Silly me. I don't know where my head is at. These pills that this Dr. Schigerr prescribes really makes me feel unwell. Maybe I'll go easy on them. But then again, they help me with my sleep." "Maybe you should! I've never liked pills Geraldine. But if Dr. Schigerr thinks they're going to remedy the situation, I'm all for it. Get you back to normal."

"Geraldine?" "Huh?" "Phillip, you said 'Geraldine.'" "I did? Oh, maybe I did. She's one of the new secretaries. I always get their names mixed up." "You seem to remember her name quite well." "I do, huh? You jealous, fox?" "I most certainly am!" "Don't be. She's a dog face." "How crude Phillip. Don't talk about women like that. Well maybe except her."

Clarissa pulled herself towards Phillip and sat on his lap. Phillip caressed her face and kissed her nose. "You look beautiful tonight

Clarissa. Did I get your name right this time?" "Sure. Keep it up for a shiner. I might stay in your memory longer." "So, he really said you're okay darling?" "I lied." "You lied? Are we in the habit of lying now?"

"I don't know. You tell me. 'Geraldine?'" Phillip rolled his eyes. "But in all seriousness, He said I might have MPD." "MPD? What sort of thing is that?" "Never mind. It's practically nothing! Guess who I ran into? Maude Hauser." "Maude? Ha! Did you deck her?" "I wanted to. She nearly knocked me over at the drugstore." "Be more discrete Clarissa. If this comes back to the firm, I won't hear the end of it."

"I tried! But she kept asking a bushel of questions and I wanted to leave." "Does she still have..." "Yes! She won't leave the house without those God awful victory rolls." "Someone should buy her a calendar and tell her it's 1954. Get with the times." "She was also wearing her dead sister Corra's fur coat. It's a good coat, I must say."

"How dreadful. But she's old money so she's able to get away with all sorts of those things." "I suppose." Clarissa laughed and Phillip pressed his fingers to her foot. "I think it's gonna live." "Oh it is Dr. White?" Phillip lifted his wife into his arms and kissed her. "Think we can make it upstairs without falling?"

"I think it's quite possible Mr. White." When they got upstairs, Phillip placed Clarissa on the bed along the cerulean satin sheets and took off his robe. He slipped off Clarissa's garments, pulled down his underwear and slipped into bed. "You think you're up for it tonight darling?" "I'm always ready when my husband is."

Later that night, Clarissa felt flushed and made her way to the bathroom. She grabbed a small towel, dipped it in cool running water and ran it across her face and neck. While turning off the light, she felt a surge of energy run through her fingers, causing her to fall back against the toilet.

She put out her hands, watching them in disbelief as they glowed. She nervously returned to bed, snuggling up against her husband, slowly kissing his neck. He placed his arm around her and she fell asleep. When she awoke, Phillip was gone.

She grabbed the telephone and rang her friend Agnes. It had been a while since the two got together, but Clarissa needed a friend. "Hello?" "Yes, is Agnes there?" "'One moment.' Hello?" "Hello Agnes, it's your friend Clarissa." "Clarissa! What a wonderful surprise! How have you been?"

"Oh you know, just keeping busy. And yourself?" "The same actually! The children have finally recovered from this bug going around and are back in school so I have so much free time now." Clarissa could hear the innate desperation in her voice. "That's why I was calling you. I thought maybe you'd like to have some coffee and cake and chat for a bit?"

"That would be lovely! What time were you thinking?" "Noonish maybe?" "Can you make it at 1? I have some art coming in and I want to make sure I'm here when it arrives. Would that be alright?" "That sounds just about fine." "Oh, I'm so glad you called Clarissa. I really need an ear." "I do as well! I'm excited to have you over!" "Likewise doll." "Okay, I'll see you at 1." "Perfect!"

Clarissa realized she didn't have a store bought cake so she pulled out some flour, sugar, chopped nuts. She pulled out an apple spice cake recipe and began to skin some apples. She kept getting distracted by the thoughts of Riva and the apparent hallucination she'd had the day before. "Why am I in here making a cake from scratch? My!"

28

She placed the cake in a mold and into the oven. Once she placed everything in the dishwasher, she opened her phone book and looked for the number where Riva was staying. "Hello?" "Hello! My name is Clarissa White and I don't mean to intrude, but may I speak to Riva?" "Yes, of course. One moment." Clarissa took a deep breath, picking at some batter on her apron. "Hello Mrs. White how are you today?"

"I'm well, thank you Riva. I don't mean to bother you, I was just wondering when you were thinking about coming back?" "Is there a problem Mrs. White?" "No, not at all. And I'm not rushing you. I know you're with your family and that's lovely. I just needed to speak with you." "We can speak now. Most of the family is out, and I'm just here with my daughter."

"Riva...if I ask you something, do you promise to keep it between us?" "Of course Mrs. White. I always keep it between us." "Not even Mr. White?" "If you wish Mrs. White." "I do." Clarissa held the phone close to her mouth. "Riva, have I ever...uh...well this is certainly hard to say." "What is it Mrs. White?"

"Have I ever struck you? Hurt you? Anything like that? Please be honest. I won't be upset if you tell me." There was a long pause. "You there?" "I'm here Mrs. White. I was taking the phone in my room." "Okay." "Mrs. White I'll be perfectly honest..." "Please do Riva. I really need you to be." "The reason I asked for some time away was because...and don't take this the wrong way Mrs. White..."

Clarissa felt faint-hearted, afraid of what Riva was going to reveal. "Go on." "...Was because of what you do at night." "At night? Can you elaborate?" "Yes Mrs. White, of course. Well, after midnight, you begin to wander the house..." Riva paused, looked around and lowered her voice.

"You begin to wander the house and you..." "Yes? I what?" "You start to talk about strange things." "Strange things?" "Yes, strange things! Like you're not yourself. It's very peculiar, to say the least. Mr. White has been very worried about your state so he asked me to keep an eye on you. That's why I started to stay over for a few months here and there."

"What was I doing? What do I...do?" "It's all so peculiar Mrs. White, that's all I can say. You seem to be engaging in conversations, as if you're somewhere else...except you're home... like you're sleepwalking. But I thought it was innocent. Except, each night it got worse. Until one night when I...OH NO Mrs. White I can't tell you all of this! It's too much. Mr. White will let me go." "Riva, the only way to help me is to tell me the truth! I believe you."

"You have some kind of uncanny energy. That's the only way I can describe it. Something comes out of you, something supernatural. It's like nothing I've ever seen before! Mr. White told me to keep all of this to myself and to take some time off because I was so scared, Mrs. White. I really enjoy working for you both but it started to get really bad."

"I just can't believe it. I mean, I do believe you, but this all sounds too fantastical and..." "Mrs. White do you really want to know?" "Yes Riva! That's why I'm calling you! It's important to get to the bottom of things." "You have some kind of POWER. Electricity, or some kind of energy. It comes out of your fingers. Your eyes...they turn completely violet...glowing. Like an animal in the night. I have to stop myself from screaming. It's unnatural." "Unnatural?"

You struck me with your fingers...the electricity or power or... whatever it is...it struck my legs and hands. I have broken skin. My shoulders are bruised and sore. I tried to get away but you...Mrs.

30

White... you attacked me." "Oh my goodness!" "Yes! I hid the bruises. I began to wear turtlenecks because people would suspect something was wrong. Mr. White said it was happening to him too!"

"Phillip said that?" "Yes Mrs. White. He said that when you slept, the bed would tremble. That you would levitate and you...flew around the house." "Flying?! Why that's absurd! Why I..I..." "That's what I said! Until I saw it for myself. You FLEW around the house like a small bird! In and out of the rooms, at times, staring at me as I hid beneath the covers.

Mr. White and I were terrified. We wanted to call the police or a doctor but we were unsure how helpful that would be. So he found Dr. Schigerr." "Dr. Schigerr?" "Yes! He's very keen on the occult and spiritualism. Mr. White told me that Dr. Schigerr had studied many books on the subject from Ernst Jentsch, Sigmund Freud and Eleanor Dorsey. Luckily, a good friend suggested him for you."

"What friend?" "I'm not sure Mrs. White. But you've been better ever since. I needed to take some time to see my family because it all became too much. You understand?" "Riva, I had no idea. I'm so sorry! Please, take as much time as you want and need. You'll always come back to a secure job. I'm so thankful you were able to tell me all of this. My goodness, I don't know if I'll recover from this news!"

"Please don't be upset with Mr. White. He loves you so much and wants the best for you." "I'm not upset at all. I have to go now Riva. You've been a great help!" "Please Mrs. White, call me any time if you need me." "I surely will Riva. Take care!" Clarissa was mortified. She rushed towards a mirror and touched her face and arms, mortified.

She looked down at her hands and feet. "How could all this be?"

She remembered last night, the incident in the bathroom and she felt compelled to cancel with Agnes and call Phillip, but it was far too late for that.

Clarissa placed the cake on a tray and let it cool. She sat down and closed her eyes. She began to do breathing exercises as Dr. Schigerr had suggested but then realized he had been lying to her the whole time. She then remembered that two times in a row, that young lady at the drugstore handed her a white bag outside.

Clarissa didn't quite realize what was happening but now she grew suspicious of everybody. The doorbell rang. Clarissa jumped up and wiped her sweaty palms on her apron. She untied it and tossed it in a bin. When she opened the door, Agnes embraced her and said "I brought some white wine just in case!" She let out a chortle and nudged Clarissa.

Frustrated, Clarissa slammed the door. "It smells delicious in here! You didn't go ahead and make a fresh cake, did you?" Agnes snuffled around. "Lemon? No! Apples...Apple Spice Cake! You didn't! Yummy!" Clarissa didn't know how to hide her feelings. She nervously began to brew a pot of coffee and shot half smiles to every story Agnes decided to say.

"So, when I found out there were wasps, I didn't want to disturb them! I feel so bad but the exterminator is coming next week!" "That can be quite a challenge!" "Yes, you're right! Oh Clarissa, I was just waiting for a moment when you wanted to call me. I know you've been so busy. We ran into Phillip so many times, Junior and I. He said you were so preoccupied and I was so happy to know you had a job now. Such a modern girl. I envy you!"

"A job? Yes! A job." "He said you were working at a doctor's office uptown. How exciting!" "It's just paperwork and answering phones and it's not a doctor's office it's…it's The Dorsey Merchant." Clarissa cut Agnes a piece of cake and poured her a cup of coffee, trying not to look like she was lying. She kept her head down as she spoke and she felt ridiculous entertaining it. "Milk and sugar?" "I actually take mine dark with no sugar. The cake is already so sweet!" Agnes dug her fork into the cake and took a bite.

"Oooh! The Dorsey Merchant! How fancy! So many women we know work there! Good for you!" She quickly grabbed a napkin, and after a few bites, spit the cake out. "Is something the matter Agnes?" "Salt! There's so much salt in that! What were you thinking? You know you have to taste to make sure it's sugar! That's an honest mistake! Oh, and it looks sooo good!"

"I must've been distracted. I'm so sorry!" Clarissa felt scatter-brained. She took a look around and remembered she had some frozen meat pies. "I know you love my meat pies and I just happen to have two. I always keep them around just in case! It'll only be an hour or so. I don't have a microwave!" "I have time darling, no problem!"

She brought Agnes over to the sofa and pointed at her hair. "Your hairpin is quite exquisite. You're always so put together! I love that." "Clarissa, that's such a compliment! Junior likes my hair done every day. You're lucky." "I'm lucky?" "Yes! Well, you don't have such a dominant figure. Phillip is so laid back. And so are you!"

"Well, it's important that we be. Life's hard enough, isn't it?" "That's absolutely correct!" "How's your mother?" "My mother passed away, Clarissa. I thought you knew that?"

"Was I supposed to?" "I beg your pardon?" "I mean, I didn't know. I wasn't told anything. I would've reached out." "You were at her funeral." "Oh, yes. Yes that's right." "Clarissa are you alright? You seem a bit...off." "Just the stress of the day. That's all. Phillip's been working late nights and sometimes I get lonesome. But nothing to lose sleep over."

"Phillip told us about that actually." "About what? You do know I have a phone?" Agnes laughed. "Of course! But we often see Phillip out and he keeps us up to date with how you two are doing." "Does he? I bet he does." "Sure, sure. Normal stuff. He says you've been having night terrors. Who doesn't, right?" Agness sipped on her coffee. "I think I WILL have some sugar after all. But please make sure it's sugar!"

Clarissa made her way to the kitchen. "What did he say about my night terrors?" "Oh, just that it's been keeping you up at night. I have some tea for that, if you'd like some?" "Sure!" Clarissa placed the sugar on a plate and handed it to Agnes. "They say that night terrors come from health issues. Have you been feeling unwell lately? You look a bit flushed."

"I have my moments Agnes. But I have a question for you, if you don't mind." Clarissa grabbed the coffee out of Agnes' hand and put it down. "I need your full attention!" "Shoot!" Clarissa sat close beside her and put her hand on Agnes'. "What are your feelings about... The Occult?" "The Occult? Oh my, that's a real question huh?" "It is! I know it's sudden..." "No no, it's okay. I think it exists to some degree. Some hocus pocus can't all be fishwife's tales, right?" "Right."

"People claim to have seen ghosts and little green aliens, so I suppose demons and such aren't far off. But all of that scares Junior. We can't have a conversation without him flying off the handles. He's Catholic, you understand. But I keep telling him that The Occult has something to do with saints as well. I'm really not well versed in it, but sure, it exists I guess."

34

"Do you think demons can possess people?" "Gee whiz, what a question! I thought I was coming over for cake and coffee, not a seance!" Agnes giggled and put more sugar in her coffee. Clarissa once again took the cup out of Agnes' hand and placed it down on the coffee table. "I just get curious, is all. But it's okay. We can talk about something else." "Clarissa, why are you so curious about such otherworldly things?

You've been watching old B movies? Are they spooking you up?" "I think I may be flying around my house like a witch!" "Ha! Aren't we all!" Agnes let out a big laugh and accidentally spilled her coffee on the coffee table. "Oh shoot!" "I'll grab a rag! No big deal sweety!"

Clarissa served Agnes and herself the meat pies and she avoided the wine for clarity. When they were done, Agnes gathered her things and met Clarissa at the door. "It's been such a pleasure Clarissa. I know you may think I'm just a boring housewife with no sensibility, but sometimes it's nice to have someone to talk to. Sorry about the coffee spill!" Clarissa gave Agnes a sincere hug and whispered, "You're perfect just the way you are."

Clarissa closed the door and put the plates to soak. She opened her white bag and pulled out the bottle of prescription drugs. She walked over to the bathroom and flushed every one of them down the toilet. Flustered, she sat at the edge of her bed and said "What's really going on?"

CHAPTER FOUR:

RUBY

My obscure personality was shifting like volatile tectonic plates. I was the wall of glass everyone threw rocks at. "Go back to your country!" They'd yell on the street. They wanted to see who could crack that wall first and if I'd come tumbling down for a cancerous audience. The function of all my forces seemed anything but enigmatic; a boulder rolling down a hill for everyone to see. It's sad that often I'd remark to my family, "I didn't ask to be born." I was misjudged and portrayed like a secret caricature.

They saw me like they saw a possum: common and without a thought as to the intricacy of colors or detail. Where the possum came from or where it was going. They saw a moving target. They knew, even when they didn't have a weapon, that they could shoot it down. I dug a hole for my shame and sunk it underneath the bathwater. I didn't want to speak Chinese and I avoided eating noodles or steamed rice. I wanted to walk the floors of the mall with blonde girls, laughing and buying pretty floral dresses, covered in high ponytails.

I wanted pizza with extra cheese and pepperoni and I wanted to pop in videos of Sixteen Candles because Molly Ringwald was everything. "I can't believe that I gave my panties to a geek." That always cracked me up. My parents who worked hard to make ends meet, I never told them about how boys stood behind me in class holding their dirty fingers to their oily temples, slanting their eyes and making pee pee in coke jokes. I wanted to die. In what fucking world was I going to a prom with a hot guy?

I couldn't make sense of my weight as it fluctuated; I was short and they said I smelled like curry. Like curry! Privileged white kids who have no sense of Geography. That kind of shitty thinking was like forced heat in a room. I wanted to do what the other girls were doing: throwing up after their meals, measuring their waists. I wanted to be the girl next door.

I spent copious amounts of time in my room chained to my fears. Life was like The Real World: San Francisco that played around the clock on MTV; how everyone tried to decipher Puck but all he was, if anything, was a ball of rudeness who liked to spit and be dirty. I couldn't understand that. Though I was nothing like him, that's what people saw when they looked at me.

I was disgusted with myself for a very long time. That's why I quite easily got into that car. I didn't need to be coaxed or given the greatest reason. I saw a way out and I took it. He was much older, tattoos across his lower arm, dark brown eyes. His jeans were worn and faded and his hair was long and soft. He put his hand on my lap and smiled. No one ever did that. I felt compelled to put my hand in his. I felt like such a free rebel, smelling his Marlboro Lights and Avon cologne.

The nicotine flicked around in his car and I felt myself taken completely. I felt like an adult, like someone who could have a say. If we went to his house, I could say "Hey let's open these shades" or "Would you like me to make you some pizza or "We can order it. It's whatever." I giggled to myself at the thought of being someone's sweetheart.

It was like destiny because we never got red lights, the music was low and they were playing "Zombie" by The Cranberries. I was in love. I realized I might miss "My So-Called Life" that night but it was worth the skip. "I might even shower with him. But with my underwear on. No, that's..I don't know." I thought.

An Asian-American lead, how sophisticated and surprising. What a box office turn out, they all showed up to my movie. I felt like the new girl in the John Hughes movies who didn't have to wear chopsticks in her hair with an accent. The most beautiful girl in the world that Ruby would be. Not some floating princess jumping from cloud to cloud. But something changed this trajectory.

I got my period. I knew I was late, but I forgot. The air was slowly being let out of the balloon. He would see that I was just a 15 year old girl with zero experience and he was going to drop me as fast as he picked me up. I looked down and I crossed my fingers, hoping my pink pants weren't going to soak in red. "Fuck!" "What's wrong?" He asked. "Nothing." I said quietly. He patted my head like a dog and then put both hands on the steering wheel. He was going faster.

"Can you slow down and maybe...um...pull over so I can get some... um...pads for...um...I'm so like, embarrassed to say but like..." He laughed and looked down at my crotch. "It's that time of the month? Mmm, I love that baby." I rolled my eyes and deflated. I couldn't breathe because I was so flustered. He switched radio channels and suddenly street lights and houses became noisy insects and the smell of farm life. He put the windows up and I held on to my book bag.

Nervously, I went into my bag trying to find a pad somewhere but he savagely pulled the bag away from me. "What are you looking for in there?!!! Are you trying to hurt me?" I was stunned. I started to feel so many things: fear, dread, panic but I tried to keep my composure as good as a young girl could in a car with a complete stranger. "No, I was just looking for a pad. I'm sorry." He stared at me and then threw the bag over to the backseat. "Why don't you climb back there so I can smell you?" "Smell me?"

"Yeah! I want to smell that virginity. Are you a virgin?" "NO!" I blurted out, lying through my teeth. I put my hands over my pants as if that were to magically make the blood stains disappear. My adrenaline was pumping. I burst into tears and all I could say was "I want my mom!"

He began to punch me. He swerved all over the road and then finally parked along an empty area. His fists were entangled in my hair like violent branches.

My sight went blurry, my hands desperately feeling for the handle. I screamed with all my might, managing to get the door open. The pain on my forehead was so intense, the blood covered my face. I could taste the broken teeth mangling my inner cheeks. His panting disgusted me, the smell of sweat, nicotine and gasoline. I yanked so hard, that a ball of my hair curdled in his fist.

I fell out of the car and began to crawl into a grove. My nails dug into the stony soil, my knees bruised. I couldn't see anything and so I wiped the blood from my face with my scraped arms. When I looked down at my hands and saw the blood I began to scream. A flock of birds disturbed, jolted out of sight. I passed out.

I woke up in his backseat, his large body pressed against my small frame. My awakening seemed to intensify his orgasm. He thrust deeper into me and I screamed and screamed. He held his dirty cracked hands over my mouth and he came. He tied the condom delicately and tossed it into his pocket. I laid there numb and ruptured. He pulled me out of the car by my legs. I felt my youth split in two. He searched for the pieces of tooth and then he placed them in a small bag.

He frantically wiped down the car and I laid on the ground motionless. All I could see was my mother. I wanted to reach my arms out to pull her in. "Run!" I heard and I did. I ran into the woods and ran for my life. I couldn't see where I was going but I felt it: the wind, the darkness, the coniferous forest engulfing the ominous space. A limited amount of freedom I had to make for. I could make it...I could make it and get away from him.

A bullet grazed my shoulder, another hitting my neck. Then two other bullets piercing my skull. Two more to my back. My life pulled away from me, and there I died. He wrapped my body in plastic like he had done this before. He then put me in a freezer and left me there for six days. On the seventh day, he put me into the trunk of his car and then threw my body into a river.

A beat. And then another. And then another. I could feel my body contort and my arms crashing into the cold air like tentacles. My hair untangled from the plastic. I felt my veins pulsating, the nerve endings convulsing in fury. Each harnessed blink and then fingers and toes wiggling. The water slabbed out of my lungs and my auditory perception fell in line. I could see my brain lining rambunctiously as it struggled to dance into its pieces. So much time had passed and so much life was lost. And I still came back together.

I came face to face with my murderer. He sat at the bar drinking whiskey shots and beer, pushing peanuts past his thin lips. He'd gotten a fresh haircut, his nails still dirty hands still cracked, t-shirt with the smell of Aqua Velva after shave. A young blonde woman with too much eyeshadow and bright pink lips, kept her hands on his lap like an indentured servant. She wasn't interested in sports and didn't particularly care for the smoke and ash flying into her face.

She kept checking her phone and licking her lips nervously. "I have to go call my dad right quick, okay?" She couldn't wait to jump up and run into the restroom. She sat there peeing while she texted her boyfriend. "I'm at The Rooster Cork come get me." He replied, "I'm not coming to get you. You're playing too many games." "Fuck you then!" She responded and then rushed out to slide her hands under his arms. "Harvey, are you staying much longer? I need to get home."

I sat beside the woman and whispered, "What's your name?" "I beg your pardon?" She asked, staring me down. "What are you even doing here? Aren't you a little too young?" Harvey pulled away from the roaring television above him and said, "What did you say?" The woman shrugged and sipped on her beer. Soon after, they headed to his place.

I walked up to the second floor, past the creepy clown portrait and into a closet. He didn't even try to hide it. There my book bag was, behind some old shoe boxes. My pants were stuffed lazily into the book bag. I pulled it out and placed the bag on the kitchen counter. "Harvey, do you have a daughter?" The woman asked. She was scantily clad in her panties and bra sipping on a can of beer seductively.

Harvey threw some logs into the fire and said, "Come sit on my lap." She walked over, pressing her ass against his hard member. He ran his hands across her chest and she reached in to kiss him. She began to grind on him and placed the beer can on the side table. As she began to breathe heavily, I got close to her face. She opened her eyes and screamed. Harvey, startled, pushed her off his lap.

"What the fuck Keri?!!" Keri got up and walked into the kitchen. She picked up the book bag and put it on. "What are you doing?? Where did you get that?" "I dunno Harvey. You tell me. You like little girls?" "Whaaat?" "You like little girls right?" "Why the fuck would you ask me that?" "Don't get upset Harvey.

You always buy me little girls' undies and you like me calling you Daddy. Do you like it when I call you Daddy?" "Okay, yeah...so what? Why are you acting weird Keri? Are we fucking or what?"

"Who's Ruby, Harvey?" "Ruby? Are you fucking crazy? I don't know a Ruby! You're going fucking nuts Keri. I knew you were psycho but not like this..." "Shut up Harvey. Shut up! And answer my question. Who is Ruby? And don't give me one of your half ass answers. Are you fucking little girls Harvey? You picking up little girls and raping them? Like you did to me when I was 15?" "Okay get your clothes on you nut! I'm taking you home!"

"Harvey we're not leaving. Who is Ruby?" "I don't know a fucking Ruby!" "Then why are you so defensive?" "I'm not!" "Sure you are! Whose backpack is this? Is this Ruby's backpack?" I had managed to possess the young woman. I felt her long legs and her swanky arms clutching to the book bag for dear life. I could sense the fear but I couldn't stop. I needed him to remember me. To remind him what he did to me. But I also didn't want to put her life in danger. So I pulled away.

She fell to her knees in tears. Harvey sat there in shock not being able to collect his thoughts. He was sweating like a pig and then ran up the steps. He walked into his room, took the rifle off the wall and went back downstairs. Keri began to scream. Harvey pointed the gun underneath his chin. "If you don't stop screaming I'm gonna blow my fucking face off! I'm serious!" Keri looked on in trepidation and told him to stop.

Keri covered her eyes. When she moved her hands away, he was standing there. He ran his fingers up and down the rifle and laughed devilishly. He struck Keri across the head and she slumped over. When she woke up, she was tied to a pipe in his basement. She was shivering from the cold.

She had her panties stuffed into her mouth and Harvey stood over her. He had his rifle placed against her head. "You're a slut Keri. You've always been a slut and you always will be. Don't you have a family? Good for nothing hookers just askin' for it! Well I'm gonna give it to you!" Harvey pulled the trigger and her head exploded against the cement. I couldn't do anything about it but just stare in disbelief.

I sat on that familiar passenger seat while she rolled around dead in the trunk. He turned on the radio and lit a cigarette. "Zombieee... Zombieee...Zombieeeeee" He quickly switched the radio off. He drove for an hour until he reached a construction site. It was snowing pretty bad but he didn't care. He dumped her body, got into his car and left. He went to a nearby liquor store and bought a bottle of vodka. "Hey lemme get a pack of those. Thanks pal."

When he got home, he took his pants off, played with himself while thinking about Keri, then poured himself a drink and sat in his chair. My backpack sat there in the middle of the living room and he stared at it for a long time. He placed the drink down and fell asleep. He woke up to banging on his door. He jolted up and walked to the door in his underwear.

"Put some pants on Harvey for God's sake! This is serious!" It was an older woman in her early 60's. "Mama what's going on?" "No no no Harvey this ain't time for games. Your neighbor Kurt called me...said you had Keri here last night." "What? No way! That shit is always accusing me of something."

"Don't lie to me Harvey Duane Brandt!!" "I ain't lyin' to you mama, I wouldn't..." "Kurt said ya'll was at the bar and then she came over. He said he never saw her leave...said you had another mysterious bag in your trunk. Oh Harvey, I need you to tell me the truth or I can't help you." "Mama what are you talking about?" "HARVEY don't fucking lie to me!! I've had enough of your bullshit! You're disgusting! And you're messy.

How about that Asian girl that was driving with you?" "What Asian girl?" "You think I'm stupid Harvey. You think I was born yesterday? Your mama wasn't born yesterday! You got some kid helping you now? Your daddy is really upset. He says he won't be able to help anymore. It's too much Harvey."

"I ain't do nuthin'! You lost your mind Mama with all due respect!" "Oh is that so? Then what's that? Where did that book bag come from?" "It's none of your business!" "Liar! You better burn that bag and you better meet me and your papa at the shop. NOW!" Harvey, still drunk, managed to get dressed and got into his car. Pulling out of the driveway, he saw his neighbor peer through the window. "Fucking Kurt."

CHAPTER FIVE:

BLAIRE

"Reality Sets In" are not the right words. The state of conjunctures that shocked me into life seems like a downplay. "Abuse" is a word thrown around to put a name to a face; to narrow it down. Detective work to say the least. When a lonely traumatized woman enters a room, no one sees the invisible scars and that's how they like it.

That "caterpillar turns into a butterfly" or "this too shall pass" bullshit seems to trickle down daughter to daughter. Heart lines are erased and fragmented pieces are suddenly compartmentalized so we have a victim, a diagnosis and a conversation.

A Protection Order and a choice of words in front of a judge, but my kids were never truly safe. I had to work and so, he came around a lot and knew how to manipulate the system. I grind my teeth at night to the sound of cars passing by, sometimes thinking about if he's watching me, trying to tame me into his unknown.

He thinks I have all his postcards and love letters from high school but I burned them all. They say nothing hurts more than birth, but the worst that hurts is never the most that it is. It's a delusion doctors say to make you feel warranted and accomplished for opening your legs. Literally.

And when I pull off cords from televisions and strike my children to the beat of what I was taught, to teach them a lesson, I hope secretly they never hate me. That I will grow old and need them and they will not scoff at me and let me wander the streets. Cup after cup of coffee and shift after shift seems to give me a possession of my due diligence; so they can say "She worked hard" and "At least she gave us what she could." But the agony I faced, staring down at the decline of my mental health, was substituted with gifts and large Christmas trees that lit up to hide the dark.

The bathroom door was locked for only minutes at a time as I gathered my thoughts. A glass of orange juice struggling not to slide off the sink counter; counting my pills like dollars. I felt weighed down like a stubborn IRS manager with a pitchfork. "I want to dye my hair pink," she says. He wants to secretly dress in girls' clothes. He says it makes him feel like he can be his authentic self. The other one has night terrors and I have to hold him in my arms until he falls asleep. Once upon a time, I was freely dancing on top of bars with my tits out, glorifying my youth and pouring shots into my mouth while I giggled with older men.

How did I meet this man? Did I think I was not going to get older? I could feel my past memories kicking my teeth in: Why did they buy me Barbies? Why were these dolls so fancy with wedding dresses selling us the fucking dream? I was a child. I needed to know this wasn't it. I wanted to be on the top bunk because I was once fearless.

I liked pillow fighting with my older sister and watching shows early in the morning without a man chasing after me with a knife. I wanted bowls of cereal and table talks with my mom who fried ham and eggs and blared the radio for us Sunday Mornings.

Instead, my existence dripped down like rain corroding walls, filling pots, softening ceilings with streaks of reddish brown. Instead his fists played around with my face like firecrackers on the fourth of July. POP. POP. POP! I couldn't escape the molded heat of his breath and the alligator dictatorship in my home. I gave him the gifts that were my children and he white knuckled it while drowning my soul.

Two strong veiny work hands around my neck, the coarseness plummeting into hot water. I broke the furniture: every lamp and picture frame and the kids saw that. They saw me display my most vulnerable anger and I regret that. But in the moment, I shined like a blazing towering fire, showing him who was boss for at least five minutes.

He seemed to think it was funny and I could see the lines form around his face while the light of day pierced through the lime green kitchen window. "Don't step on the glass" I told them, with tiny feet jumping over each piece.

I sat on the sofa with my eyes transfixed on each line of self-help books, marker in hand trying to fix this life. We didn't have a television: that was broken. We didn't have a toaster: that was broken. We didn't have a coffee table: that was broken. We didn't have hearts: that was broken. There was a first time..that I decided to leave.

I didn't make coffee so I wouldn't wake him. I whispered to the kids, got their bags ready and on what seemed like the coldest day of the year, I packed them into a car and took them to a motel. I barely had enough so it was very cheap, where the locks barely locked and the beds seemed more worn out than me.

The kids were peering through the windows like they were in jail and I couldn't forgive him for this. For allowing me to be in this state. For knowing that I'd have to return eventually. What did they know? Three kids, like puppies clinging to each other while I chewed off my nails. What was I to do next? I didn't want to call my parents and burden them. The more I thought, the more the smell of cigarettes from the rug burned my nose.

I only had a tank of gas and I sat while they slept, on a chair blocking the door. I could hear the working women leaving their rooms for the day, Johns getting into their SUVs smoking Marlboro Lights and pulling out of the parking lot. I paced around in the little space I had and thought... and thought. Before it got dark, I piled the kids back into the car, we got dollar burgers and returned home. My hands were shaking, opening that door. My palms were sweaty and he was standing there in his ripped jeans giving me the side eye.

"Where'd you take my kids?" He screamed. "Where'd you take my fucking kids?" This time, dislocating my jaw with a can of paint and ripping my hair out. "Were you trying to leave me?" He spit into my eyes and knocked me to the floor. The linoleum, paint, the thick air, the sweat and blood. I could taste it all.

The crescent moon swooned as I was laid on the bed like a frightened cat. He forced himself on me as the walls closed in, the depression rattling me like an old cage. His moody thrusts impaling me, sliding inside me like an angry snake, sinking its teeth into my stomach. He came inside me like he was giving me a reward.

He alienated me with his phony jealousy. I fell. I fell. I fell for it. I kept falling. I stood up and then he'd knock me down. I'd put my hands up and he'd knock my lights out. I yelled at him and he overpowered me. I ran but he caught me. He always caught me. The devil was in the smeared lipstick and the many times I said "YES."

There was a time when history wasn't moving so fast forward and I was understanding him beyond the superficial. A time when I lit up at his arrival or at the attention he gave me. I thought my femininity was a powerful prowess and not a bait and switch. I'd come to find out it was a torture chamber and a masochist. "So tell them you fell." My mother said early on.

She wore her stupid flower hat and her glasses and she crossed her legs at the doctor's office. She'd pass me a mint and a reader's digest and say "I told you. But you wouldn't listen. So tell them you fell." I could hear the galloping of horses; the race to the finish line and what it took to get there even if their hooves hurt. The threat was that if they didn't, they would get a bullet to the head and then be replaced. What a sad second place.

After years of tension and feeling like an actress out of work, I left. I took the kids and moved in with a friend. I knew before I got there, it was only a matter of time before I was picked apart for breathing. No matter what I did, there was an issue. My kids didn't get a meal sometimes, they were often accused of stealing, of touching the remote, of saying things they weren't supposed to say. This was my fault for deciding this for them. I only wanted to give them a better life.

The restraining order was limited. The judge seemed somewhat reassuring, but my husband looked at me like a pitbull that hadn't been fed for days. My husband: what a wonderful play on words. My husband: auburn hair, dark cold eyes, long trunk legs, long torso, an impossible glare. How could I be such a foolish fish, who've seen hooks all my life and still take the bait? How could I flop around in his arms knowing I was dinner and yet be so elated to fill his stomach?

****

The stores were full and it seemed like the day had grown feet and went running. There was an early doctor's appointment for Ashton, his ears were bothering him and he was coming down with a bad fever. Hazel turned 13 the day before and she kept egging me on about the pink hair. Matthew almost burned down the apartment making scrambled eggs. While nothing was ever ideal, we were managing this time. We finally had our own place, I was working a steady job and he told me I could keep the car.

Aisle 5 and I was looking for the generic brand of mayonnaise that tasted better, then off to get a gallon of milk and cheese. I pulled up to my apartment, the sun attempting to set slowly and I fumbled with my keys and opened the door. The silence was deafening. I figured they'd be in their rooms doing their own things.

"Someone help me bring up some bags." I yelled. Silence. No TV, no radio, no one arguing. "Hello?!" I looked at the clock and it was 5:46pm. I suddenly got a bad feeling in the pit of my stomach. One of those feelings you can't shake. Like when you're sitting in the theater and you see the girl stepping onto her porch yelling "Is anybody there?" and the entire audience is throwing popcorn at the screen because they already know what's about to happen. That feeling.

Then I heard his tremulous voice and it startled me. "If I can't have you..." He said. My heart skipped a beat. I didn't know what to do, so I put the bag down and there I saw it.

On the kitchen counter a gun was sitting there. I felt a tremendous heat tickle my spine, spreading up to my neck. "Where are the kids?" I asked, almost knowing the answer. I walked into one of the rooms and fell to my knees. My daughter was shot dead. She was in her bed with her headphones on, listening to The Beatles. There was a magazine of Mademoiselle right-side up. My son Matthew slumped over in his room with blood across the floor and wall. I couldn't feel my jaw...I couldn't make out words. My youngest, in the bathroom, drowned in the bathtub.

A Nightmare, Come To Life.

I dove my hands into the water and held him close to my chest. I smelled his hair, I felt his lifeless hands against my breasts. What animal would do this? I allowed this to happen. I lost it in that moment. I ran towards my husband, wanting to rip his eyes out. Wanting to destroy him for what he did. I thought I was free. I thought they were free.

And then one after the other, gunshots to my shoulder, my neck, my back. I dragged my body towards the door, the streak of blood, pieces of my skin in my hands. Then another shot to my head.

HE KILLED ME.
HE KILLED MY KIDS.
I ALLOWED THIS TO HAPPEN.

"And then what?" I said to myself. I felt my feet dragging from street to street. The lightness of my being drifting, my immense guilt like a carcass full of ravenous flies. I wasn't ready for this.
Each street sign got smaller and smaller until I couldn't read a thing. Then it got dark. It got really dark and my fear spaced into the plains and the fields. It felt like the moon was not only watching me, vigilant and not trusting of my whereabouts, but ready to squash me.

I looked behind me and then in front of me. I couldn't figure out which way was what. I couldn't figure out what all this meant. I panicked, I'll admit. There was no usual creature comfort. I said to myself, "Maybe you should run. Maybe if you run, it'll all make sense and you'll eventually end up somewhere." But my sadness didn't allow it. I felt weighed down. But I picked up each leg and I ran. And I ran. Until I crashed into something in front of me.

I rubbed my head and I tried to catch my breath. Who do I feel sorry for? Was it myself? My children? His ability to be so exact in his revenge? Whatever I crashed into, banged me up good. I could see each gunshot speak to me, telling my bones to return. The loudness returning to quiet, the veins telling me that it was all going back to how it was.

I bet the blame game was intense at the funerals. "We told her to leave him." They'd say under their decaying yellow teeth. "But she didn't listen." They lived their lives of unrequited misery like a staged drama set to music. My mother would be the first to mourn me in shame. The times she called and I didn't answer because I thought I had it all figured out.

It was in the fervent pleasure where my womanhood blossomed, and in the many times we'd argue for the sake of it. It was where my first kiss came from, his hands pressing against the small of my back at my cousin's basement. Now I was blowing towards the wind and not against it, in what felt like a daydream soaking up my humanness. I was no longer a progress of life but needing to feel that proof of existence.

In 20 years, they'd rip away blood soaked carpets saying "this place has good bones." No one would be eager to read a news clipping about the incident, and the furniture will come in one by one. Families will move in and out, dogs running around sniffing our continuum, their astute noses runny from the awareness.

They didn't buy me a large headstone, but that changed years later after several rounds of therapy and my mother, finally accepting that it wasn't my fault. Family photos of the kids will sit over her dining room until she dies, always speaking of them to strangers as present tense. Every Christmas dinner and the sound of "Hark the herald angels sing..." reminding her of my time as one of the sheep in the Christmas play when I was six.

I hope I won't see this monster in this purgatory. Whether it is a purgatory or a Hades, and if I must suffer for my sins, I hope it isn't beside him. Or maybe he will be spared. Maybe he did everyone a favor by getting rid of me. Maybe he doesn't need any repentance because he was doing good work. What if I had to endure an eternity of seeing my children die those horrible deaths because I couldn't make it home on time? Or because I didn't have the guff to leave a man who was so terrifyingly normal.

The answers that you receive might not be the ones you want to hear. Maybe I will wander through darkness until I am granted some form of penance. What I would give to lay on my mother's lap and tell her that I loved her. That she would run her fingers across my hair and face and say "You sure make dumb mistakes but I'm so proud of you girl."

Maybe there's a heartbeat and I'm back to seeing my kids grow up. "Ashton, come to Mommy. Let me heal your ears baby. Come sit on my lap baby. You're so beautiful." I'd never tell him that he looked like his daddy even though the nose and eyes are identical. Just to hold my baby in my arms and see him grow up to be beautiful and sweet. And even if he didn't become a doctor or lawyer, I'd be okay with it.

Matthew, you're allowed to be who you are. My sweet beautiful handsome angel. Put on that dress, that lipstick, find out who you are on your own terms. No matter what, mommy won't judge you. I won't kick you out, I won't get upset and make it all about me. I won't. I'll let you be you and I won't treat you differently because of it. I love you so much baby.

Hazel paint your damn hair! I give up! You're gonna grow up to be just like me. I saw that instantly but I tried to fight it and fight you, so you wouldn't head in that direction because I was afraid of my mental health issues and it affecting you in the future. It really fucks with you cuz' you think you're on the right path and then you can't get out of bed. It's so dreary and you want the shades closed and it's just not gonna get better sometimes. Sometimes.

But maybe that's your cross to bear and maybe you won't turn out like me or maybe you will and that's okay too. I'd give anything to hear your voice, even if it's "Mom please stop shouting!" or "I hate that shirt!" Anything to hear your voice my lovely. I miss my kids. And now that I'm gone, it feels like a long time coming to think about all of this. But I really, really miss them.

The answers that you receive might not be the ones you want to hear, but they could heal you. I think.

"Can you hear me spirit?" A voice called out. "Can you hear me?" Blaire felt as if she had lost her footing and dropped into the ocean. The external elements all around her, the deepest depths like extraterrestrial compounds; she could feel the salt entering her body, every breath like saline, crashing into her, weakening her. "Can you hear me spirit? If you're there, make your presence known."

Violently jolting, Blaire lifted her arms trying to grab onto anything. Her nerve endings tactile and acute, fleshing out formations of fingers with every increased friction. Her nails dug into the front and side of a table. "I'm here." "Spirit?" "I'M HERE."

CHAPTER SIX:

RACHEL

"That's him." I said. The parallel lights between the double mirror, the detective's hand on my shoulder, a filtered vision. I held my ice pack over my bruised cheek and all I could think of was my father waiting out there. I didn't want him to panic.

They finally let me out of that blistering room and I fell into my father's arms. The icy hoary walls triggered me. I got into the car and I placed my paperwork beneath my feet. "It's gonna be okay Rachel." My father said. He always seemed manically hopeful.

But I knew that it wasn't going to be. This wasn't the first time. It was the toxic Boy Culture of my time. They got away with everything. They could fuck anyone, be with anyone. They always got away with it. The cops know. The judges know. The lawyers know. Another buck spent.

And as I predicted, I was tortured on the stand. It went on for months. Republicans slammed my defense. What the fuck was my defense? A 19 year-old college student trying to live her life in a dorm? Trying to get through her Liberal Arts Degree? I was painted a whore, a monster, a person who was Un-American for exposing the good ol' boy. And so the story goes, they get off scot- free.

The first few weeks after the trial, classes didn't seem safe to me.

I couldn't focus. The story had been in the school newspaper and my name was dorm fodder. The guy who almost beat me to death, raped me in his car in the college parking lot...his name was up in bright lights for the game. He played his holier than thou football and the college won, crowds came wearing his name on their shirts. Little kids with his number chanting "We love Robert Shireburg!"

Young women with "Listen To Her" buttons sat outside with their compact tables speaking candidly about what happened to me, but no one cared to listen. The words fell on deaf ears and even they eventually forgot. CNN told the world what happened to me but no one cared. I had to leave the college after all the debt I had, because as they put it, I was a "disruption" to "their campus."

Then it all started up again. I was working at a store and he waited for me with some of his friends. They ridiculed me and I could see the lights from their phone screens in the dark saying how they were going to trash me all over the internet. So for safety purposes, I bought a small handgun. Every night I waited for them to try something, but they only taunted me.

I called the police several times and filmed the incident, but all they did was tell them to stop. They knew I was the "rape girl" and they didn't want to be associated with that, so every encounter was few, far and in between. To them, Robert was a football king and I was only looking to taint his image. I eventually left my gun home, and ignored them all together.

Until one night, when they followed me as I drove off. I could hear people yelling obscenities and I didn't even realize it was them until I rolled down the window and heard their voices. I tried to call my mom but she wasn't picking up. Then a sudden violent impact, and my car spun out of control.

The story had a panel of experts trying to decipher where I was, talking over each other: what I was doing and where my body went missing. Truth was, they crashed into my car and I flew into a tree. Robert and his friends removed me from the car, stripped me to my bra and panties and forced themselves on me, one by one.

I know no one wants to hear the gory details, all the truths that make a rape. I know it's so microscopic and taboo to think that it could happen the way that it does; but people have this preconceived notion of a "neat rape" where they line up, thrust and leave.

That is far from the truth. It is a fabrication and has nothing to do with what the victim has experienced, and everything to do with how the act is perceived. So many people don't believe victims because they don't see rape as something tangible.

Americans seep themselves in zealotry and religiosity because it tames their spirit. Their cult of sport and hunting, pot roast dinners and immaculation of men inoculate the ugly truth and keep their evil pristine. And until it happens to them, they can't sympathize or cope in realism. They put away the fractured pelvis and the ruptured uterus; the disruption of a cycle by large members penetrating, destroying and weakening with each entry. The dry blood along the inner thigh and the self-congratulatory smirks.

They feel as if the victim is ignominious; that she serves part in her humiliation and has the stealth to live with it. It's quite a feeling to lay there with screams you never knew you had coming from the pit of your every being. Helpless hands scratching away at polyester and muscle. Until the heart gives out and can take no more.

I wanted to get married. I thought I was going to have a house full of strong daughters. I could see myself watching as they graduated, each one with their degrees. Each one to move on to something great. I thought I'd marry Gabriel Filman. We'd move into an apartment and then as soon as one of us made it to the big time, we'd buy a decent sized house and we'd be so happy. So much sex, so much love, so much history. Those perverts ripped that from my grasp.

Then they pulled up their sweatpants and buried me right there. They didn't go far, they didn't drive me anywhere. I was lying 10 feet from the spot my car crashed at. Yet no one cared to find me. That story was huge. The ratings were huge. So many people felt so sorry for me. They were so angry at what happened to me. They wanted so badly to find justice for me. And then they moved on with their lives.

Six years later, a class of 2nd graders came to plant seeds. It rained a few days before, and Mr. Parker thought it was the perfect time to sow seeds. They were simple seeds for flowers and the class would return to it in a week's time to watch the results grow. I felt each seed and I was reluctant to let anything grow there. So the class came back a week later, and there were no flowers. Mr. Parker looked around and made sure they were in the correct spot.

They were. He decided he'd go the following week, but that whole month was rainy and wet. Still no flowers a month later. Mr. Parker then abandoned all hope and decided to plant seeds next year in a spot that could possibly sprout flowers. He figured the soil was bad, but something told him to come back alone. He came back early one morning on a Saturday.

He got on his knees and dug his fingers into the wet earth. I pushed back. He reached in and pulled something out. He fell back horrified and immediately ran to his car and called the police. The same police that had ignored my pleas, made their way to the "scene of the crime."

It was a grandiose announcement and detectives and cops, confused and lazy as they were, stood behind a makeshift podium to pat each other on the back. Each channel broad-casted the news as if they were stunned. Reporters were eager to get a piece of the story that was ALREADY out there. The real horror was not my rape. The real horror was not my murder. The real horror was that the city that I grew up in...that I loved....had betrayed and abandoned me. And there was hell to pay.

For years, kids drove their cars into those woods and had sex; then they'd pull their pants up and dash out as if no one had died there. Some of those boys came on the dirt and pushed back into their chargers and raced into the night. Some of them brought liquor and sat out there spitting and romancing and fawning over innocent girls. I raked against the metal and crunched the branches so they wouldn't form.

I appeared ghastly in a ripped dress, blood dripping from my head as a reminder of the hate this city once had for me. The kids would scream and rush out and for a while no one came back. I was a folklore. Though my bones were buried at some granite mausoleum in that god forsaken city, I was still back to square one. I could still feel the heat and the girth of those pigs, joking at my expense, growing inside me, burying me and then going back to their dorms. I was not happy.

A group of middle-aged "white witches" decided to do a seance there. They wanted to meet me. I wasn't in the mood. They placed rocks and crystals and made an outline with chalk and I was quietly observing. I sat beside one of them, admiring their tenacity. One of them had short black hair and she seemed to think she was conjuring up my "spirit." She jolted and spit and rambled, and the others seemed genuinely frightened.

Then she pointed feverishly and said, "She's there!" One of the guys covered his eyes and the youngest girl there got up and walked over to the spot. I couldn't believe the nonsense. But the one I sat next to, turned his head and looked straight at me. He couldn't process what he was seeing and skirted backwards screaming, "She's right there! Oh my God she's right there!"

Suddenly, the entire group began to chant my name and asked me to appear to all of them and I was not having it. I closed my eyes and when I opened them, they disappeared. They'd all gone back home. What a relief.

The following weekend, the guy who saw me, returned back. I'd lived my life to die by the hands of men and now it was a man who was finding me. I didn't like that. I didn't reappear to him. He sat by himself, praying to the trees and the sky and whatever else he could think of.

And I think they heard him. He was very audible. They could hear his sincerity even though he wasn't much of anyone to conjure up spirits or whatever. But I did hear him loud and clear. And so did a few others.

CHAPTER SEVEN:

UMEZDA WICKER

I didn't want to believe in ghosts or in any demons. And every dream I had with an evil witch screaming outside my bedroom window, I cried on the skirt of my mother. She quipped that I watched too many horror movies and that I should focus on school. At night, in the rustling of the wind and the flickering lamp posts, my sleep was interrupted. Interrupted by shadows and creepy sounds and it was interrupted by my overactive imagination...or so, I believed. I was a lonely child and it seemed I'd be like that all of my life.

The sadness inside me came from beyond the womb. My mother had suffered a great deal while carrying me; her parents both died and she was struggling to cope and make ends meet. I would watch my mother sitting at the table with a loaf of bread wondering where our next meal would come from. She suffered badly from back pain from years of spousal abuse and she relied heavily on painkillers.

I remember "It's A Wonderful Life" was playing and my sisters were carefully planted in front of the television and the glow lit my way so I didn't stumble upon any shoes. Because I was terribly clumsy, I always wobbled in and out hurting my feet or knees in which I developed a genuphobia.

I made my way down the small hallway along the wooden panels and I'd see my mother lying on her bed in the dark and I'd always check to see if she was okay. I would wiggle her wrists and then push her shoulder a bit. Her pillow would be wet from tears and she'd put her arm around me and I'd fall asleep beside her.

When I became a teenager, I realized that there was no darkness to be afraid of. The monsters were in the light. Memories don't die, they fade like watercolors. What was larger than life was smaller than it seemed.

Years and years can pass and you can look at the watercolors and see the technique. And like all art, it is subjective. But memories are not subjective. They exist because they were and are. We all come to find out, sooner or later, that competence and mastery have nothing to do with personal experiences. When you look up fast because you swore something passed right by you, like an elusive shadow or when you're tossing and turning and the ceiling seems to fall into you. Things like that.

I tasted gravel walking from a store, after buying some candy. I loved red licorice and gummy bears and there was a store that sold penny candy. I was walking home and two people pushed me from behind. The gray sky finished up and my mouth was full of dirt. My candy clenched in my fists, I lifted myself and didn't look behind. It didn't matter who pushed me, it only mattered that I got out of there. I learned that day that having what you want was always followed by a punishment. And all the while, I kept quiet of my traumatic dances with life.

The fever I had about getting older was that people changed their looks, their faces, their ideas, their points of view, their styles, their mentality, but if they appreciated humanity they would never hurt anyone intentionally; that if empathetic and coming to terms with their darkness, they could cure themselves of unintentional evil. No one is a victim without their perpetrator.

One cold night, walking near the Atlantic shore, I found myself alone and vulnerable. The waves kissing each other, enamored, crashing against each other. All the jellyfish gliding in a blueish hollow, only dangerous to the touch, but harmless otherwise.

The salt in the air stunned my lungs, my fingers digging into my coat pockets. Alone is non-existent when everything is surrounding you at every moment; every smell and every sound coming at you even when you're not doing a thing. "Alone" is a made up word. We are never really, truthfully "Alone."

That night, the beginning of my adulthood began under my hands. I placed my palms against the wet clay sand that was lightly dusted with snow, closing my eyes. And the pneuma in every fingertip lit up as if I were touching every flat surface, every sidewalk, every crushed foliage and every fertile structure.

And I heard the voices of women coming forward of all shapes and sizes and different walks of life, pleading with me to speak on their behalf. It wasn't subtle like sitting across someone or understanding their stance. It was like maximum energy, a volume of jolts persuading me to fall over and into a collision of feminine lacerations across the skin. SHE was EVERYWHERE.

My pupils were struck with white lights, my retina slashed into scopes of dotted lines. Evolutionary characteristics splashing into my peripheral view. Each premeditated word on every side of the gold spectrum echoed into my ears, fervently clawing its way into my psyche. It was as if they were using telescopes to look into me.

And as furious as it came was as soft as it left. Every voice caressing away into the daylight. I heard each woman's denotation of events, palpable and striking. But they couldn't hear themselves as loud as I could hear each and every one of them. As if the sun had decided it wasn't going to give off heat or light until God Himself said so. I gave them longevity to a short eternity; and a moment to reclaim what they lost. THEIR LIVES.

I sat across a pastor, and as he sipped his espresso and smiled awkwardly, he already had a speech prepared for me. He patted his hands responsively, so proud of himself for sticking to his rehearsed lines. He was universally exactly like every religious fanatic who fancied themselves "normal" as to his way of speaking and being. The dogmatism was so thick that I could have walked into any church at any decade and I'd be sitting exactly right across from him.

He was his own deity; the conceit and the plummaging of his sectarianism with the cross. He believed his own words because he deemed them to be true which is the chaos of man's inevitable demise. "God doesn't cosign this" he spewed as he took another swig of his espresso. I looked across the room and noticed his family in every picture: a million views of pumpkin patches and straw bridges, big floral hats and baby's first steps. Cherry picked bible verses to illuminate everyone that came in and out of that room.

His tie was sitting slightly over his bulging stomach, as he leaned over me to say "I'd love to pray for you." He reached out his slick sausage fingers that smelled of coffee and cologne and touched the back of my hands that were folded in front of me.

With his lips pursed, he began to pray loudly so his wife could hear it, who was right outside the door. His wife, who pretended to do everything and know nothing, who hung around the church like a dark cloud, while her children played with instruments and terrorized church members in the coming years, paid close attention to what was going on so she could unleash her tongue to every person willing to listen, or unwillingly be subjected to her woefully topsy-turvy reign.

She lowered her head and mechanically closed her eyes. "Heavenly Father..." He began, as he tightened his grip against my hands. His fingernails pressed against my crotch. "Please deliver us from evil and please Lord, help this young man understand that he is your child and not the child of Satan...and Lord help him know that no matter where He is, You are."

He pressed his forehead against mine and continued. "Whatever demon of clairvoyance that has come upon this child of God, I cast it out in the name of Jesus. I CAST IT OUT NOW IN JESUS NAME!" I focused and mumbled basically everything he said, my heart in the right place, wanting to be free of anything that didn't belong inside me. The pastor repeated his rebuke. And as he did, he opened his eyes slowly as his forehead was still pressed against mine.

He leaned in and kissed my lips softly and then pulled away. "Amen!" And then he put his hands on both sides of my shoulder and squeezed tightly. "He nodded at me as if speaking in a secret code, getting off that his wife was right behind me, right outside that door. His perversion in the midst of what was holy and intimate made me sick.

I pulled away, thanked him and got up to leave. His wife smiled slyly at me as I walked past her, as if she were terribly concerned but I didn't smile back. She walked into the room, patted her husband on the back and grabbed his espresso, cleaning up after him in her usual nosey manner; scanning the room for what she didn't know and what she did.

As I got into my car, the pastor honked and got out of his. I put my window down and looked over his shoulder as his wife cut through me like a knife with her pretty accurate perception of what her husband was up to. I wondered sometimes how it felt to be a prop in someone's life.

How she could be so obviously zealous and yet so ignorantly willing to go along with his charades. Then I noticed how brand new her car was and how expensive the church looked and it dawned on me that her existence was based solely on being his "loyal" wife. Chilling.

The pastor smiled and looked quickly behind him as if he were in danger of getting caught doing something only he knew he was doing. He was hardly a predator, as predators have prey and I was nothing of the sort. He spoke in a whisper and I rolled my eyes.

"Feel free to text me buddy. I'm always here for you." His whisper turned into a hyper whisper. "I'm free Monday after 4pm if you'd like to pray more." He put his hand on my shoulder and squeezed it.

Then he walked over to his car, got into it and drove away. And in brush strokes, his DNA on my skin spoke volumes about his escapades and the stolen sermons; how he would be discovered, his mouth over a teen boy while he stroked into a green glow in the dark condom. His wife barged in, doing what she does best: ACTING surprised, flouncing around and throwing her hands in the air, screaming like a stabbed cow.

I see how he dies, slouching over a chair while his wife sleeps soundly; she's 69 and he's 71. The heart skips...skips...then stops and his fists clench. His wife wakes up, finds him there and genuinely sobs over her husband, truly sad to see him go. The sham was over and how delicious it was for her to play it out until the final scene. She whimsically spews how forgiveness was key to her matrimonial longevity.

That every scandal was replaced with mercy and grace. And three worship leaders with over-sized pink and gray sweatshirts cast their voices over a live band who was no doubt forced to be there. His five children in a row, like sitting ducks...like Republican pawns in their finest black toe to toe attire, pretending to be shocked and in awe. Reminiscing and usurping the snakery and nefariousness of their kin.

They'd unite to rule over their church with hardly an iron fist, keeping the disgraced legacy of their parents intact. The rumored racism and the up dos, the charges on credit cards paid for by the supposedly unsuspecting congregation who are more complicit than they are true believers. Following devious men who lie to them over and over and they just hand in their life savings like indulgences to be spared from hell.

Sadomasochists who, when the time is 7pm, flock to sing and dance and slither around on the floor, without an ounce of knowing what HOLY and CHRIST is. A spectacle for one another like mating salmon who flop around and die. But if they're happy, hey?

As I drive away, my mind races over to his forehead against mine, his lips against mine and I'm no better than he is. Perhaps I am easy prey. Or perhaps he is.

CHAPTER EIGHT:

ROSALIND

I didn't know what I was doing. I was out of body. I was out of my mind. The drugs did that to me. My children were always home alone without any food or clothes. My mother was tired of me calling, asking her to come over to take care of them. "Rosalind, I'm not coming! Get your head on straight and leave me out of it!" Of course she would come over now and then, but she was getting older and being overweight didn't allow her to make these trips or help the situation.

She was dealing with lung cancer and the kids exhausted her. She loved having them around, but not at the expense of my issues. Lord only knows how many times she kept me out of harm's way while still putting food on the table and raising kids. She once chased me around the kitchen when she found a bag of coke in my room. I couldn't sit still cuz' I couldn't bare the truth. She had truth in her eyes and it was hard to look at her. A Saint.

But when she did, she'd bring bags of groceries from her own pantry, and she would cook and clean and text me every two seconds to see where I was at, what I was doing, when I was coming home. The needle in my arm was my authority figure. It had seduced me from day one.

I couldn't recognize myself in the mirror. Every man I came in contact with was going to get my marked up body in exchange for some crack and heroin. I tried. I tried switching over to weed laced with some other things so that it could maybe make me a better mother.

But every time I fell into my addiction, I was in the abandoned house, eight blocks from my kids, shooting up and fucking. No warning, I'd just leave and not come back for days at a time. I was not looking to get sober at all. I loved the feeling it gave me, I was invincible; thrilled at the concept that something so small could be so powerful. That it could momentarily erase all of my worries and pains. But the temporary wasn't good enough. And I was so sick of hearing otherwise.

I was breaking my mother apart. She was walking around with her purse when I was there. I saw the pain in her eyes when she'd try to have a conversation with me and I would just nod off. There were days when she sympathized with me, holding my hand and explaining how this was taking a toll on her and the children. If she went to the bathroom, she would take her purse with her or yell out to one of the kids "Come on up and bring me my purse. Make sure nothing falls out."

Then there were days when she would not come to her door, sitting silently in her recliner while I banged and screamed "Mom let me in!" I could see through the blinds, the tears rolling down her cheek. I could see the breathing tubes and tissue boxes and her rabbit slippers tucked to one side.

The many times I had to lie to her and say I was going to get better, but then I'd snort coke in her bathroom. I was so disrespectful and it was killing her. I was killing my kids. I was killing myself. One of the many breaking points was sitting naked in a tub, in an abandoned apartment, a needle stuck deep in my arm, my nose bleeding and me sobbing to a stranger that I traded my youngest son for a hit. My son was only five and was sitting in a drug dealer's house getting raped while I got high. I was disgusting and could never be forgiven.

I stood in front of a judge for the 6th time, and she asked me to stand up straight. My hair was messy and wet and my blouse had dark spots from dropping a hot spoon on it. She banged her gavel and said, "Miss Sumley, do you understand the words coming out of my mouth?"

I just shrugged and laughed, rubbing my arms and aching to sit down. "Miss Sumley, do you realize you left your five year-old son Austin to be sodomized for a number of days?" I put my head down and licked my lips.

"Miss Sumley, do you realize that the people who you left Austin with were convicted felons and rapists? Do you understand that a witness saw you exchange your son for drugs? Is that correct Miss Sumley?" I shrugged and slammed my hand into my stomach. "Miss Sumley I need you to answer yes or no please."

"Yes!" I shouted and looked down in shame. "Miss Sumley I want you to know that your son is currently in South Clark Memorial for injuries pertaining to the actions you chose to partake in, do you understand that? Did your council make you aware of your actions Miss Sumley?"

"What's he in the hospital for?" I asked lazily. As if they were talking about another woman or another careless mother leaving her son somewhere unsupervised. I was just as outraged as they were. But the drugs in my body seemed to speak for me, and the negligence foreshadowed my existence even as I was being sentenced for human trafficking and a slew of other things. I just didn't understand the severity of what was happening.

I sat in my jail cell, trying to focus and suddenly a woman cracked me across the face. "Wake the fuck up bitch, those are your kids!" She struck me again and I fell to the floor flabbergasted, entangled in a fight. The cold bars didn't keep me from understanding empathy. I was just sorry I wasn't outside getting more drugs.

Every passing day and every time, they'd let me out because of overcrowding. I'd sit in my halfway house contemplating, plotting my way to a drug. I knew I was being tested so I kept my cool. I'd attend AA meetings but the stories were so boring and silly that I just didn't give a fuck. There wasn't an ounce of remorse or a plan to get back my kids.

My selfishness was imploding. One day, I called my mother to see how she and the kids were doing. My sister picked up. "Rosalind what do you want?"

"Hey Mimi, I just wanna talk to momma...that's all. See how she's doing, how the kids are. How are you?" "The kids are okay. They need their mother but you already know that. I'm just fine. But you need to know. So I'm just gonna go ahead and say it even though I know you don't care. Momma? She's no longer with us."

Nothing hurt more than that. That rocked my world. It felt like an airplane had slammed into my house. Just chaos and destruction. "What?" "Yeah you heard me. But since you wasn't calling anymore from jail and nobody wanted you at the funeral, we didn't tell you." "Nobody wanted me there? What? Not my momma!"

"Cut the shit Ross. Please cut the shit! You are a piece of work is what you are. Momma died because of you. She was sick already you asshole!! And you knew that. She was sick of this life. And

God decided to take her... finally. To relieve her from the pain you caused. So don't act so fucking surprised and hurt. Take this time to apologize to your kids, getting clean and winning them back."

My sister Mimi hung up and that's how I found out my mother had passed away. I sat in my room sobbing, hoping to stay sober and not being the horrible things she said I was. I sat there for hours and then walked all the way across town to my mother's house. I sat sweaty, outside her door feeling numb on her front step. My sister Mimi was inside but she didn't care. I got it. I understood the frustration and anger. Even the hate. I was a terrible human being.

Eventually, she opened the door and sat out there with me. She put her arm around me and kissed my cheeks. "I'm a terrible person for saying all of that on the phone and I'm truly sorry sis, I really am! The last thing I want you to be, is sad.

I know that you're struggling with addiction and all these demons surrounding you but what you did to Austin is unforgivable Rosalind...UNFORGIVABLE. You sold your son, you do know that? For a bag of heroin...it's disgusting! DISGUSTING. Fucking terrible sis! Your kid getting passed around like that, all the psychological and physical damages...that was all you. But you're sick and you need help and I know you'll get it.

However, if you fuck up one more time, it's better you stay away. It's better you push that needle deep into your veins and die than hurting one of your kids. Another black woman, a fucking statistic...dead in some warehouse or some roach motel. You need to do better. Want better. You have destroyed your life...do you hear me Rosalind Ivy Sumley?

Those kids do not deserve what has come their way. They're resilient, good but they are damaged because of it. And what was it all for when our mother had to see all of that while she was alive. We're supposed to lift our mothers up, be there for them and give them what they need. She never needed any of this Ross. It is truly terrible. I mean it!

You have turned into our father, a no good scumbag piece of shit who beat momma every day of his natural life. You have accepted that gene and you are here ruining your life and the life of everyone else. I challenge you to change. I challenge you to give a fuck about someone other than yourself for once. Can you do that? For yourself and for your children?"

I'd never felt more enticed to change. I felt like I needed that kick in the ass. My heart was pounding in my throat and I put my arms around my sister. "I...I need your help Mimi. I need your help sis cuz' I can't do this alone. I'm drowning. I feel like...I'm drowning! I know that if I try to do it alone, I'm going to fail. Mimi, I can't fail again."

"I know little sis. I know. I know it's hard. But do it for momma. Do it for Tamika and Austin and Shawn. You know Shawn is rapping bars? I rather he be reading books and going to class but yes ma'am! He wanna be a rapper like Ye-yo, God rest his soul. He sounds really good too. They are growing up so fast sis.

I got them going to church and doing things with them. I wanna make sure that although they see evil everyday, they know God is good and God can make away for all of us. Cuz' none of us are perfect. Especially not you! But eventually that forgiveness will prevail, just not in the ways YOU want. But it WILL prevail, you best believe it!"

I was on probation and it was really hard to get my kids back. The courts believed I would endanger them again and no matter what

I said or did, it wasn't a possibility. But I fought hard. I had a court date with a mediator who helped me speak to my kids and I was sent into a room. I waited for what seemed like forever, and a man from Child Services sat across from me. He didn't smile and only made small talk.

Then finally, my children walk in. My daughter Tamika who was now fourteen, my son Shawn who was fifteen and my eight year old son Austin. "Miss Sumley please be advised that you may not touch your children or speak of anything that will cause them harm. We have 20 minutes and once that time is up, you will be escorted out. Please do not address Austin. You may speak to the other two but the courts find that any interaction with your son can hinder him more than help him. Are we understood?"

"Why not?" I screeched, knowing the truth. But I wanted an undeserved redemption. I wanted to reclaim something I destroyed. Tamika rolled her eyes at me and barely listened to a word I was saying. Shawn looked tired and older than he was. Austin seemed sad but happy to see me. He didn't say a word, but I knew he wanted to hug his mommy.

After the visit, I reached in to hug Shawn. I felt like I could express that I was sorry by doing so because it was my right, but he pushed my arm away and said "You disgust me. You're not my mother. You're a drug addict trash box bitch!" Tamika swatted at his head and said, "Stop! That's our mom! Like it or not!" They disappeared and I was left alone to contemplate those words.

"You're a drug addict trash box bitch." Wow. It felt like my soul was ripped right out of my body. But I deserved to be called worse.

When I was escorted out, I got into a taxi and headed straight to my old drug dealer. Turned out he was in jail and it was a kid named Ricky Dicky. I couldn't inject myself faster. I felt the drugs jet through my veins like fireworks on the fourth of July. My high was so intense that I ended up missing my probation appointment.

I just didn't give a fuck anymore. Then I met Wilson. I used to see Wilson around here and there but I always thought he was kind of a loner. He offered me some dope and I couldn't resist. It felt like I had a partner in all of this and I remember crying on his shoulder telling him that I needed to be the best mom I could be.

Wilson had a semi-dilapidated house and we did drugs all day. He asked me if I was willing to have sex for more and of course the answer was "Yes! He wasn't bad looking and I wanted to stay high. He instructed me to take off all of my clothes and to hang my panties on his dresser. I did. He slowly pushed inside of me and fucked me on the floor. Then he stopped midway. I didn't understand why he would stop, but he did.

"What did you say your name was again?" He asked. Suddenly, it felt strange. I felt truly alone for the first time. Naked. "Rosalind, why?" "Wow that's a pretty name. I like the name Karen. I also like the name Sharon. I also like the name Maron. Names that match. Names that feel good. The motherfuckin' name game!" "Yeah, I guess." "Go ahead and spread your legs wide. Spread them until you can't anymore. Are you flexible Rosalind? Ugh, I rather call you something that rhymes. Is that okay?"

"Um, I don't really care." "So go ahead and spread your legs. Wider!" He was fucking freaking me out. "Why do you want me to do that? Aren't we gonna keep fucking?" "Yeah we are, but I wanna see what you look like down there. I bet you have a really dark pussy. I wanna know what you're workin' with."

"Hey man, I'm feeling really weird about all this." "No! No no no

Rosalind, don't feel weird. We're friends." He came towards me and kissed my lips. "You're so beautiful. I like your hair. I like it cuz' it's natural and you don't do anything crazy with it like some girls. I like your lips. You kiss great." "...thank you..." "You like it kinky?" "It depends. How kinky we talkin' about?" Do you mind if I put a hammer inside you? Hold on, I'll be right back."

"Hold on, wait...no...I don't want..." Before I knew it, Wilson jumped on top of me, holding me down, pushing my legs open with his knees. He kept laughing into my ear and I spat on his face. He took the hammer and swung it, striking me once on the head. I heard a crackle and a gush of blood streamed down my face and neck. Completely panicked, I began to scream, fighting him off.

He tried to force the hammer inside me, but I fought him. I fought with every breath. I could feel the cold hammer smeared in blood, trying to penetrate me. My legs were pushing back and forth until I finally kicked him off and rolled across the floor. My head throbbed and I tried to stand up but he stomped on my back and then slammed the hammer across it. I turned around and swung my fists and they hit his chest a few times but he overpowered me. He struck me once...then twice..then three times on the face while he forced himself on me. When my head split open, he came. He screamed "ROSALIND!" And then pulled out. He seemed ashamed and embarrassed.

He dropped the hammer beside me and kissed my lips. Then he fell on top of me and started crying. "You were the prettiest one. You really were!" He cried on me for a few minutes, then wiped his tears and left the room. Later that night, he returned with a gun and some knives. He pressed the gun to my head and said, "If you move, I'm gonna blow your lights out Rosalind."

But I was already dead. He put the gun away and started to drag my body, stuffing it into a closet. Four days later, he decided to re-visit the closet and have sex with my decaying body. Once again, he came inside me. He kissed my icy blood curdled lips and put his head close enough to what resembled mine and laid there laughing, telling me about all the women he had raped and murdered:

"Aneasha was so weak. She was so desperate. I put her to sleep because she needed it. I dumped her in the river and the cops didn't even care." He let out a sinister cackle and continued to speak as if all of it were normal. "She was a black girl with green eyes and I found that fascinating. So pretty. Not as pretty as you. You were the better looking black girl. But Sharon had big tits and I like tits. You were pretty flat. But who cares? You're dead. Next!" He pulled up his pants and sat beside me.

"The cops don't care about no black girls! Fuck you talkin' bout?! They told me! Yeah bitch, they said 'SO WHAT?' You know how many times ya'll be disappearing around here and they just at the corner store tryin' to book these dudes for selling loosies? Ya heard? All those kids in Atlanta and those kids in Chicago. I'm not sayin' I know what happened to them, but it's pretty self-explanatory right? Cops don't care! Sometimes some of those narcs get their dimes from me!"

It was revolting how his eyes followed the blunt he was cutting open, running his tongue along the edges while he told me his mur-der stories and his conspiracy theories about lizard people and how restaurants poison us slowly when we order fast food. "Yo, that's some weirdo shit in this government. Listen to these rappers sis! They spittin' real talk!"

After lightin' up, he'd shove my body deep into the closet and closed the door. I could hear three more women doing drugs with him, laughing and choking and being bludgeoned to death. Two tossed in the closet like me and the other, rotting in the bathtub. He stopped story time with me and started having story time with them. After me, it was a single mother named Harland Cooke who was struggling with substance abuse. She was a prostitute; age thirty-nine and she had six kids in the foster care system.

Ashley Biggams Scott was eighteen and was studying to be a registered nurse before she turned to hard drugs. The third was a prostitute named Bianca Teller, age forty-one. Bianca left behind three daughters. Those three daughters: Moriah, Deena and Kierra were responsible for protests that led the cops to our bodies. We all had badly decomposed and my sister Mimi had to identify my body. She stood over my body in The Coroner's office. "Baby sis." She never forgot that moment for the rest of her life.

Wilson Fabian Butler was charged with the deaths of four women but was not yet linked to the other eighteen he had murdered along the way. He was sentenced to death but died of a shanking in the shower. His first victim was a sixteen year old white girl from Minnesota named Kelly Freimont. That same year, he murdered a 14 year old black girl from Minnesota named Georgia Quaid and another unnamed girl in Chicago for money.

The following year, he murdered an eighteen year old black girl from Utah named Golden Raymonds. After that, Leslie Hobber, Sarah Lynn Rodriguez, Alicia Goley in the same year. After that, he decided he wanted to be creative and move to a state where he'd kill women with rhyming names:

Kissie Carter, Missy Leafgreen, Karen Leamer, Sharon Oatsvall, Maron Gadowski, Meisha Slaughter, Keisha Redding-Moots, Aneasha Peterson, Lakia Miller, Destiny Vaccarezza, Justine Henderson and Crystal Divers.

At a Black Lives Matter rally, Bianca's three daughters held their mother's name high, along with Harland, Ashley and mines: Rosalind. They marched down the streets with our names yelling "Black Lives Do Matter...we must do better." I never got to do better. I should have, but I didn't. But I felt the love. That these women were supporting other women. Lifting their name on high.

A young man named Chris walked up to the podium at that rally and lifted a sign with a picture of his sister Ashley Biggams Scott. He stood there, taking deep breaths, his sister's picture raised over his head. "My beautiful sister Ashley Biggams Scott was taken away from us too soon. She transitioned when she was 16 and we were all so proud of her. Black Lives Matter. Black Trans Lives Matter. Ashley was taken too soon. Please do not forget her name. Say Her Name."

The crowd chanted back, "Black Lives Matter! Black Trans Lives Matter!" He lowered the sign and kissed the photo. "We miss you sis." That same day, a picture of Ashley was posted on Sympathizer News and was ridiculed that she was considered a female victim and not a male as her driver's license suggested. The panel sat there for an hour debating over her gender and sexuality as they laughed, panning to before and after photos.

There was a raucous union of ridicule emitting through the screens of millions. A victim of violence but blatantly disregarding her tragic death. They then went on to dismiss each victim, implying that because most of them were prostitutes and drug addicts, they didn't deserve their sympathy.

Women from impoverished neighborhoods that had no business being inside that house with that man. They also pointed out the mental health issues Wilson had, followed by pictures of him in his youth, laughing with friends and his brief time in the armed forces.

They questioned whether he knew what he was doing; and as long as black women were dying, they were just:

Casualties of WAR.

CHAPTER NINE:

SPEAK TO HIM

Clarissa sat quietly, looking around the room for any sign or book of The Occult. Dr. Schigerr waltzed in, waving and sitting behind his desk. "I'm pleased you were so eager to have another meeting. What changed your mind?"

"I never said I wasn't going to come back, Dr. Schigerr, I was simply taken aback by your approach the last we spoke." "I can certainly understand your concerns. It's not easy to face this head on, but we can do it together." "I suppose." "Are you alright?" "Alright? In what way?" "You seem a bit...out of sorts."

"Oh yes, I met with my aunt earlier and she gave me terrible news. But other than that, I'm fine. I'm strong enough to manage." "Wonderful. Not the news of course, but that you can manage. That's always good to hear. May I ask what the bad news is, if you're in the mood to share and don't mind?"

"I don't want to burden you with any of that, Dr. Schigerr. I'm here for something else completely." "Oh?" "You say 'Oh' as if you believed that I would never find out." "Find out?" "Yes. Why I'm REALLY here." Dr. Schigerr shifted in his chair, adjusted his tie and pulled out his notepad. "Don't bother writing this part down Dr. Schigerr, I promise you it's not that captivating." "I didn't pretend to think it was..."

"What you and my husband have schemed up is absolutely berserk and a violation of my privacy. Not to mention involving me in any esoteric balderdash you've both concocted. You see, I've found you out and I won't be needing your services any longer Dr. Schigerr. Good Day!" Clarissa got up and walked to the door but Dr. Schigerr locked it from underneath his desk.

"I suppose you'll be holding me against my will and calling the hospital to take me off in a straitjacket. Well go ahead! I dare you! You'll soon be reminded of who I know here in the city." "Clarissa there's no need for a straitjacket. Please have a seat." "I most certainly will not!" "You'll want to hear this."

Clarissa rolled her eyes and folded her arms. "I'm listening." "Please have a seat Clarissa, I promise you it's not what you think." "Oh it isn't? Really? Tell me doctor, what is it that you're really doing around here? Or should I call the police and get this straightened straight away?" Dr. Schigerr tried to move towards Clarissa but she put her hand out. "Stay away!"

"Very well Clarissa, I'll explain. I've worked with many people who have had the same 'dealings' as yourself." "Dealings? I beg your pardon?" "Psychokinesis. Telekinetic powers. Surges of supernatural manifestations. Levitation. For lack of a better word: fluttering." "Fluttering? Are you out of your mind?! Let me out of here at once!"

"Clarissa, there's no easy way to truly express what this is. I tried to pass it off as MPD or some form of Schizophrenia, as aggressive as that is; to give you a plausible answer to go home to. That it may not be alluring titles, but you could feel there was a name to what you have. Mr. White was adamant about treating you like a normal patient but also curing you of this power or numinous force."

"Curing me? Power? You both speak of me as if I'm some witch! And have you been poisoning me with your 'sleeping pills?' So I'd comply? How very calculated of you..of you both!" "Clarissa, they're not really Thalomid. Or sleeping pills."

"Dear God! What has Phillip done?! He's subjected me to you like some lab rat! Like a petri dish of conditioning, just so his friends wouldn't laugh at him?!" "Clarissa, he truly cares for you but he doesn't quite understand what's happening. I might. The pills are placebos. They don't do anything. Sugar pills. That's all."

"Sugar pills?" "Please Clarissa this is very complicated and long-winded. If you'll have a seat, I can tell you why I want to help you." Clarissa, stirred up, walked over to the chaise. "Only for a moment and then I'm leaving. You get that door unlocked because I'm going to go...right after you..."

"I understand. I'll unlock it. The button is for precautions. I once had a patient who threatened to kill everyone in my office. So I had it put there for safety." "Yes, I'm sure that's why that's there." "Now, now Clarissa, don't imply anything unpropitious." Clarissa sat down and tapped at her watch.

"When I was met with a phone call from your husband, he seemed quite alarmed, if I may be honest. He demanded to meet with me right away but I was completely booked. He said he'd pay extra and that, my darling is my only weakness. But when I met with your husband, his story sounded all too curious.

He explained that you were having issues sleeping. That you were becoming manic and that you started to display violent tendencies with your 'powers.' I've heard of supernatural pangs but nothing quite like this. He recalled that you were hallucinating, seeing things that weren't there. Not being able to remember things the next day. Going on, business as usual.

He was afraid someone would try to get you committed or hurt in any way and so he came to me. While his fear was all too real and so were his bruises and marks, he made it a point that he was very much in love with you and that you were indeed the love of his life. That he would do anything for you."

"He did?" "Yes. He also didn't want to hurt you and he never wanted it to come to that, defending himself. He explained that you were also hurting your maid Riva and that you were frightening her beyond compare. I spoke to Riva briefly and she was absolutely and without a doubt terrified of you. But let me be clear: they are both very committed to you and wanting to help you.

I handled our meetings delicately at first. I didn't know what I was dealing with. I was afraid you'd come in here and make my whole building quake, or burn lasers into my eyes like some awful sci-fi film. But when I saw that you were perfectly capable of handling yourself, I let my guard down.

Everything we spoke about in confidence has stayed in confidence, not even Phillip knowing a morsel of detail. I wanted to gain your trust. And I almost did." "I can't believe you're telling me all this Dr. Schigerr." "Indeed I am Clarissa. I want to be an open book with my process.

Last week, we spoke about going under hypnosis and it was the first time you considered it...so it seems." "So it seems?" Dr. Schigerr opened his drawer and pulled out a pack of cigarettes. He placed it on the desk and pointed to it.

"Do you smoke Clarissa?" "Do I smoke? Well...yes. Sometimes. It relieves the tension, I suppose. Why?" "It relieves the tension? Huh.

What if I told you that I bought you those cigarettes and the case you hold them in?" "I'd say you were crazy." "Do you remember buying those cigarettes Clarissa?" "I suppose that I do. I must've gotten them from home. Maybe Phillip..."

"May I ask you to take out your cigarette case Clarissa?" Clarissa grew frustrated and dug into her handbag. She pulled out the case and placed it on her lap. "Thank you. Now remove the cigarettes from the case please." "What is this all about?" "Just do it please." Clarissa pulled out each cigarette eagerly. "There!"

"Now tap that case against the corner of that chaise." Clarissa, perplexed, tapped the case until the inner hull popped out. "What does it say behind that thin sheet that fell out, Clarissa?" Clarissa picked up the thin sheet and read it out loud: "For Blaire. So?"

"You see Clarissa, you don't smoke cigarettes. You don't smoke at all. Blaire does." "Blaire? Who's Blaire?" "Do you mind if I show you something else?" "Go right ahead." Dr. Schigerr opened his drawer and pulled out a sketchbook. "Are you aware of who this is?" "What is it?" "A sketchbook."

"I suppose you're going to tell me it's mine?" "No. It's mine. You're not very good at drawing." "No, I'm not." "This book is half way filled with drawings I've done. About your vivid dreams, what you've seen, and what has happened to you."

"That's impossible, I've only seen you a few weeks!" Dr. Schigerr opened up his scheduling book. He walked over and handed it to Clarissa. Uncertain, Clarissa took it. "What's this?" "It is our schedule of appointments." "Okay?" "Open it and tell me what you see."

"This feels very odd, Dr. Schigerr. Is this another one of your tricks?" Clarissa opened the schedule book and turned page after page. "Clarissa, you've been seeing me for eight months." "Eight months?! Okay, you're completely bonkers. Completely!" Clarissa tossed the book to the side, got up and walked towards the door.

"Clarissa, where is your mother?" Clarissa turned her head. She dropped her handbag and walked back slowly, sitting down. "You're under hypnosis. You've found out...again. I've had to explain why you're here Clarissa. I've had to explain many times. It's quite alright. I'll have to push some appointments for tomorrow but I knew this was coming."

"She's just confused. You can't blame her." "Who am I speaking to?" "Stop with all the theatrics and sit down." Dr. Schigerr gulped. "Piper?" "Who else could it be, Dr. Schigerr? You men are so discombobulated with your ramblings. The poor girl is afraid! Look at how you've been treating her! Locking the door? Really? For her safety? Ha!"

"Piper, where are The Others?" "The Others are taking care of business. I happen to be free today." "Yes, but you're not looking for her progress. In fact, you're the one causing her lapses. You're well aware of that, right?" "Oh, so are you talking to me like I'm your patient now? Is that it? Cut the bullshit doc. She's your patient, not me."

"Well, you're part of her so..." "And I've already told you doctor. We are all REAL." Dr. Schigerr jolted to his phone and buzzed his secretary. "Lana, can you move back my four o'clock?" "Sure thing Dr. Schigerr." "Thank you." He pulled his chair and placed it in front of Clarissa.

"Piper, I'm going to be honest. You're starting to annoy me." "You've been annoying me since we met." "She was making such progress. The Others seem to be okay with it, so why can't you be?

90

I'm starting to believe that if we get rid of you, we can rid her of this once and for all."

"Go ahead and try." "Piper, do you really want her committed to the hospital? He is saying he is thinking about it." "Who?" "No one. Never mind." "Phillip? But you just said that was out of the question." "I never said that." "You implied it asshole." "Language!" "Fuck your language! He wants to kill her! That's what they do in Barkersville. They break you apart. Until all that's left is drool and blood."

"And that is what we're trying to avoid. I've explained it to you numerous times that if you at least...suppress yourselves, she could live an ounce of her life without seeming like a freak. The world is cruel Piper. I just want to help her." "Help her?" "That's right." "So then why are you speaking to me?" "Because you're here, that's why!"

"That's not it. You've given up on Clarissa. So it's easier to talk to Us because you can have a real conversation. But what you don't understand is that, in order for her to get better, she must face what she has head on." "And what is that Piper? Help me understand." "I don't have to explain that to you doctor. You're a man. You'll never get it."

"Try me." "Try you? Really? Have you walked in heels?" "Perhaps." "See, you don't care about her. Your jokes should be left at The Russian Tea House you frequent." "How do you know that?" "Know what?" Dr. Schigerr grabbed Clarissa's arm. "That? What you said just then?"

"Relax. All the doctors go to that place." "Careful Piper. I'm on to you." "Perhaps I'm on to YOU. We're ALL on to you." "What is that supposed to mean?" "It means that that's why Clarissa has been finding out over and over again. She knows." "She knows what? That her husband and I are trying to help her? That we want what's best for her?"

"You want a success story to write in your journals. To write that book. Will you include all of the art or..." Dr. Schigerr slammed the sketchbook on the desk. "Let me speak to Rachel!" "She's not in right now." "Then...Ruby?" "Ruby is definitely not in. I already told you...they're handling business."

"You're playing many games Piper." "Would you like to speak to Umezda?" "Umezda? Who is that? Is that another personality? Helloooo? Who is that? I'd like to speak to her." "It's not a Her. It's a Him." "I thought you said you were all women?" "We are. He's not part of Clarissa." "So then why would I be speaking to him?"

"Because he may be able to help you with her." "I'm confused. Help me?" "Yes." "Well then, go on. Connect me with this 'Umezda.' I'm willing to talk to him. "Are you sure Dr. Schigerr?" "Yes. Why? Shouldn't I?" "That's your decision." "And who exactly is Umezda?" Clarissa placed her hands on the temples of Dr. Schigerr's head.

"What are you doing?" "I'm taking you to him." "To him?" "Yes, relax." Dr. Schigerr adjusted his tie and nervously closed his eyes. He couldn't believe he was allowing her to do this. "This feels new Piper. Are you going to hurt me? I'm sorry, but I have to ask." "This won't hurt at all."

CHAPTER TEN:

SWALLOWED WHOLE

I pressed a comb to my hair, a jacket to my back and I was on my way. I'd felt her very presence next to me and I knew I had to help her move to the light. I didn't come along with anyone. It didn't seem like a group effort. This spirit didn't want that kind of publicity. She didn't want a crowd. "I am a Healer. Umezda The Healer." I liked the sound of that. I heal those that are alive and those that have passed. It is within me to fulfill my purposeful duties.

It is not White Magick. It is Gray Magick that manifests into the foundations of our spiritual realm. This woman was sore with ire. I could feel her blazing presence catapult itself into my psyche. It squeezed like a child suckling. Each season hesitated to come to pass when she manifested her motions; a muscular clay with all the impulsiveness unyielding.

There was no harmony or balance in her aura. That did not influence me. Her jeremiad did. I then placed rocks at every plane to allow the macrocosm to align her acceptance; the stark lustrous sunlight impaled the barks on trees and created creamy waves of maroon-colored beams. Her lambent invitation was aphoristic and soft as if my atoms were binding with the celestial empyrean.

I prayed so a spate of clouds would hear me without bringing on the rain. I prayed to the soil to give up what it did not ask for. It was a calling to that soul left out here to die. "Spirit! Why are you not yet in peace? What has made you stay? Where is your return?" I could see the young woman standing behind a sapling looking at me, intrigued. I pretended not to see her. She had tears running down her face that reminded me of the pain of a thousand mothers that could not be.

"Spirit? Why are you angry still? Please speak freely to me and I will not judge you." She looked around bewildered. Her hair was grit and fettling mud; something saturating her legs. Her feet were tired and I could feel the veins screaming. After what seemed like forever, she opened her mouth but something stopped her. A small child was coming forward. "Is it me that you want?" She asked. Wide eyed like a tawny owl, hands out reaching towards me too willingly.

"I was murdered in my parent's home. Abducted through a small window. I can feel his breath on my neck still. The taste of pineapple slices and warm Christmas cookies." This child slowly fell to her knees and I could see her life force turn into her affected origin, her hands like gnarled branches poking into the crispness of the air.

Her face kept changing, her lips large then small...large then small. And it seemed like something was lodged in her throat. I immediately tossed my hand out and said, "You are not a spirit, you are a demon and I will not..." But she grabbed my hand and the melancholy projected into the atmosphere. There were wallows climbing within one another. Her tortured face now pressed against mine.

"I'm not a demon. I'm a victim." And the very thought of the word "victim" coming out of her mouth, startled me. Suddenly, an older girl pulled her away and said, "Stop. He's not here to save you. Stop it!" Others began to appear and the rocks that were placed upon the ground began to judder.

The white-washed sun blazed red and my vision began to blur. I felt them topple over, hounding me with macabre stories. I couldn't hear them properly. It all seemed too much. I managed to run out of there and into my car, breathing heavily, my heart feeling as if it were going to burst. I didn't realize I was so sensitive to the deceased. The tragedies were like torrents of sadness, the callous results of an eagerly sinful humanity.
How could so many people be taken away like this? I turned on the car and pressed the gas. And as I drove away, I felt an arm reach from behind and press against my neck. Side-slipping on the road I then pulled over.

It frightened the shit out of me. I started to scream. I thought I was going to die. Then the arm loosed and I turned to look behind me. She sat there with her arms folded, beautiful. "Be careful what you ask for. And who you're asking. You might just get it." She said.

I got out of that car and stumbled on the side of the road. Instinctively, I wanted to scream. She frightened me more than those other spirits out in the woods. She seemed calm and collected. And yet it was the most terrifying moment in all of my life.

After a minute of wondering if I should get back into the car or run, I decided to compose myself. This was my purpose. I couldn't run from that. I got into the car, opened my glove compartment and fumbled out some tarot cards. I was nervous and anxious all at the same time. I couldn't see her through my mirrors but I knew she was behind me. I mustered up the courage to speak: "Spirit please... let me speak to you through my cards and I can..."

She appeared in the passenger's seat, head turned, staring into my eyes. It was like something out of a gory horror movie. Her flesh falling from her face, eyes glowing like some werewolf. Her teeth, razor sharp and hungry. I couldn't even let out a scream if I wanted to. I was terror-stricken. I was ready to die. I was ready to give into my trepidation. I closed my eyes and I pushed away from her, my knees locked. And then all I hear is laughter.

"You're so gullible. Don't fuck with magic." I opened my eyes and looked down. Piss running down one side of my leg and my jaw feeling sore. "What do you want from me?" I asked, like some 90's teen slasher flick. "To stop bothering me. Leave us alone. We're dead. So what? It's done. Right? So let it go." "I didn't mean to..."

"The fuck you didn't! You want sob stories. Well, turn on the news. The gang's all there buddy. We've all been on the front page, Special News Reports, in the back of milk cartons, pressed behind your coupons. Have you seen us? Well now you have. So go back to your privileged existence and stop fucking with the dead. Or we'll fuck with you right back."

"I wasn't trying to hurt you or fuck with you. I just felt sorry that you weren't being seen or heard in the way you should be. That's all. I was hoping..." "Hoping for what? That you could send me back into the light and I'd ascend with a halo and golden hair, winking and nodding as tears fall from your face?

Like 'Job well done!' It's not that simple. You see, what happened to me, happens to so many people. Little kids, women of all ages, sizes, colors. You can't imagine the people I've met beyond the grave. WE can have meaningful conversations because WE are gone. We do not need to be reminded of our sorrows. Because when you remind the dead why they're dead, then they suddenly feel some type of way. Don't you agree?" "I...I guess I can see... your point of view. I'm sorry to have disturbed you." "You didn't disturb me. This world disturbed me.

That we can all start the same way, formed in warm bellies; the offsprings conceived, growing the same way and that, that could be enough to unite us, and yet we all leave a different way. And it is almost always a man who takes us out of it. THAT is fucked up."

"So are you like...a ghost? Er...I mean like a feminist ghost...were you a feminist when you were alive?" "Feminist? I have a name: Rachel. But if that's the question you have, you really are some mumbo jumbo kid who watched way too many movies. Feminist? Do you even know the meaning of the word? How many women gave up their time for the cause and what happened after?

Every woman is a feminist in her own way. The ones that say they aren't, are lying. You have to be a feminist to exist and thrive. No woman is solely dependent on someone else. There are women who are eager to bullshit and say that it goes against what they believe in but then turn around and do some feminist act. They look at themselves secretly in the mirror and acknowledge it. Feminism is not just burning a bra or equal rights. It is the acknowledgment that a woman can't ever be oppressed.

No matter the century or the decade, or the men who try to silence her. Even in her silence she is speaking. The heart beats and the soul goes on. As long as there is a God, there is Feminism. That God can create the heavens and the earth and all the animals in it and around it, in the deepest of deep; every color and every breath.

And still the man was lonely. It was never in God's interest to keep the man alone. The woman would always eventually come. That is Feminism in itself. That God would exhaust Himself to create everything and still a woman would be needed. That is so beautiful and strategic.

"But didn't Eve..." "Didn't Eve do what? Disobey? The earth belonged to the devil already or he wouldn't have been in there to begin with, tempting and deceiving. The purpose of eating that fruit and disobeying God was the garden contracting to push out. Man was given everything and power to name and rule over and yet it was the one act of woman that gave course to the plans God laid out. That is Feminism.

Feminism is not the solution to problems or the root of goodness. It is not a guide or a flower that blossoms; it does not open eyes or change minds. It is an entity that is found in women and the things that they influence. I mean, nothing really changes. Eras seem momentous and then placid.

I'm a dead girl who got fucked over. That's probably the most Feminist thing ever. But maybe you're looking for some damage. You want me to give you a convenient souvenir from this ghastly Feminism from beyond the grave! I could...swallow you WHOLE!"

"I...I don't want that Rachel...please...I just want to go home!" "Yeah, go home. I'll stay back. I always stay back. But don't give me a really good reason to pay you a visit. Cuz' no one can rattle chains like I do." And just like that, Rachel disappeared. I was frightened out of my mind. But everything she said resonated in my heart. I couldn't sleep, tossing and turning trying to make sense of these turn of events. Rachel definitely left her imprint. Maybe that's what she meant.

CHAPTER ELEVEN:

THE BOY FROM PURPLE MOON

Perhaps it was the oddity in my upbringing or obvious trauma that shuffled me together; nothing more than anyone else in this entire universe. I kept to myself, I knew what streets to cross and which ones to avoid; I walked fast to and from school and my book bag was always on my back, not thrown across some snowy concrete for bullies to devour.

The street smarts were forced upon me but I was still as soft as yolk. I still needed that sweet touch of security to make me feel like tomorrow wouldn't be so bad. So I'd wait til' my parents went to sleep, and I'd pull out my favorite book from the drawer where I kept rocks and notebooks of poems. And under the blankets with a flashlight and a glimmer of the eerie street light outside my window, I'd turn the pages and read:

"Normally, on a crisp day like this where the crickets dance and the alligators have a chance, I open to a page about 'The Boy From Purple Moon.' You see we all have a dream so it seems and the silver lining is that we are children of the natural world, small and tall, some play ball, some hope under the stars, and some of us sit with imaginary wings and capes and things.

He was not an ordinary boy I suppose but who knows, who am I to second guess? His big wide eyes and puffed out chest as he ventured for the best. A story no child should forget, lest he regret. It all began one day:

His name was Willet Dime from a ripple in time, his hair the color of a chestnut or a pine. His hands were small, his nose a bit dirty. His smile newfangled, wide and long like The Sargasso Sea. And how could this be, he was alone in a forest; all alone so it seems with a pocket full of knowledge. He knew to the far-out West was the capitol castle, and to his East was a town full of peasants.

He felt more at home where humility was present. But where did he come from? A rainstorm or a comet? Did he land in a star or a reflection from a locket? Nobody knows, so the story goes, his innocent heart without an arrow and a bow.

Some say he's a boy from the great purple moon; from a great distance out, seen from any fantastical lagoon. And all of the resplendent mermaids sing all of his praises; they wait and they wait, hands up so elated. And now he is far from home, his eyelashes soaked. He rips through the dirt with his glowing coat.

"I am to see who will allow me to stay in their home, who can trust me alone." But nothing is what it seems, if you know what I mean, and if we all have dreams surely nightmares have themes. For in everything good, compliments something bad, in a land where there is pure something rotten is had.

The Eerily luminescent soul with the black tar hair, her nails sharp as axes like claws of a bear. Her beauty is unparalleled but her eyes pierce the night. She is Queen of the Lost and can give a good fright. While the reason she is forgotten is always remembered, she stands beneath dark clouds and scattered over the embers.

And every mountain quakes tremendous in fear. That she would ever walk upon them or look to their rear. For this terrible and great woman if she is to be called that, can scare such a nation like the passing of a black cat.

Willet Dime knew nothing of her name. He knew not where she lived or knew not of her shame. For he came to the world confused as can be. Looking for a friend in you and me. So then the day laid out its plans. He walked amongst the trees and land. And in their palpitation spoke, "Welcome Boy from Purple Moon." And in his walk, he met a stranger.

Someone thinly veiled in danger. A man named Sesley throwing coins. He said, "You look terrible boy. Are they not feeding your little stomach at home? Something about you seems forthcoming."

"My name is Willet, that I know. Looking for a place to rest and go. And if you kindly point the way, I will thank you three times a day." "Three times a day? That sounds preposterous! You speak like the people from a land called "Ignosterus." "I have never heard of such a name? Is it from the South, the North? Come say!" "You are an interesting little fellow. Where is your mother and where is your father?" "This interesting fellow has no interesting answers. I am alone, please help point towards Rigel or Ursa Major."

Sesley perched up and snakedly gazed. He knew there was something in front of his face. "Make a wish. Make a wish now. I am king of the wishes and I grant them somehow. Somehow is not for your very knowledge. Let me help you go home unharmed and untarnished." Willet looked over Sesley's shoulder. "I prefer to go this way before I get older."

"Nonsense dear boy, make a wish so it is granted. If you deny my services, I will have to get angry." "Anger is an emotional response. If you are not threatened, why go on?" "I see you are savvy. A wandering being. Someone who is kind but a foolish miscreant!"

"I have not broken anyone's laws. I simply desire to go my way is all." "Well, is this your wish? I haven't got all day. If you wish to go home, I will point the way." "No. Something tells me you're putting me on. I don't mean to be rude but dear man so long."

"So? Your wish is to spite me and spite my bloodline. To deny us your wish and to commit a crime!" "A crime? That cannot be, as I was walking you see. And I stumbled upon you and that is all that it can be. I have committed no crime, my witnesses are the trees.

But if you insist on my wish, here it is, listen right: I wish that you leave me alone. I wish that I was already gone, alright?" But Sesley was not a magician of sorts. He was not a genie but was in cohorts. He had other plans and he knew what to do. But he also knew the boy was astute.

"Your wish is granted, take the road up ahead. Make a left at the dandelion's tributary near the river bed. Soon you will find what is familiar to you. Your speed and it shall be waiting. Now give me a thank you." Willet shrugged his shoulders and smiled cheek to cheek. "Thank you kind sir, on my way I will be." As Willet walked on and walked on and walked on, he noticed the river bed and decided to stay strong.

And as he sat down to catch a bit of his breath, something arose from the waters and said, "You will catch your death! Do you think you can pass by these trails all alone? Without coins or an offering or a horse to call your own?"

Willet could not make out who it was. It seemed like there were humps in the river bed like logs. "Who are you? Can I tell you my name? I was told my way forward was through this little lane."

"Well, you were ensnared and certainly told wrong, and I dare you to come closer. I haven't had lunch so I dare you to be bolder."

"Please do not misinterpret, please understand. I am not here with other plans. I just want to go keep going, don't be so alarmed." "You have a glowing coat, you are not from this way. I have not seen such beauty since God molded man from clay."

"I don't know where I am, I just want to move on. I know there are others but right now I'm alone." "Is that a threat, when you mention your 'others?' Is she delicious? Your mother?" The creature now stood taller than the boy. What seemed to be wings and claws and all. "The man, he granted, one wish for me.

He said if I came this way I would be...heading onward, wherever that is. Please do not harm me, I'm not a miscreant." "Miscreant? Ha! You're just a boy. If you toss me a coin you would be saved from harm."

"I don't have a coin, please let me pass. If you let me find the man he would surely help me with that." "I don't have time for your silly games!" And in one swift swoop the creature swallowed Willet. There was darkness, there was cold. There were dead things young and old.

He passed through the teeth that were crumbled, brittle and green, passed all the fat and the throat and the spleen. And when he thought this was the end, the creature spit him out and said, "This is as far as you'll go. Be careful of men and the evil traps they set and the plots they sow.

Be careful of creatures that have malice, wearing hoods. You are unique, you are wholly good. Be gone from here! Is that understood?" Willet began to run. He was clearly near Capitol Castle.

He saw all the flags and the lights and the bustle. He noticed a girl with braids in her hair. "Excuse me Miss can you help me a bit? I'm looking for a place to eat and sit." "If you aren't a resident you don't belong.

Where is your tag and where is your swan?" "Swan? I don't understand." "This is our national animal and you don't belong. You must be from another land. Are you delivering a message to our king? If so, then his men are these." She pointed afar where the horses were rounded. Willet looked upon so cherry faced and astounded. "I'm only trying to find my way. I want to remember but I feel so alone."

"I cannot help you, no one can. If you're caught in this area it could mean both your hands." "Please Miss! Please help me, I can give you my coat. It is all that I have, this is all that I know." "While your coat is quite splendid, you still don't belong. Put this tag on and wait here a bit. I won't be long."

Willet waited and waited and the boredom this created. He counted the leaves and the plump bumbling bees and as people passed on, they grew suspicious of him. The girl with the braids had not returned, and Willet's patience was lost. He felt forsaken at every turn. "Perhaps she is busy, then I shall be on my way." But as soon as he said it, she appeared like a ray.

"Forgive me, my tardy, I brought bread and cider. A scarf to cover your face and a cygnet for barter. You mustn't lose this creature, keep it quiet in your sash. If anyone finds out, I shall be made of ash." "No worries my lady, I will honor your name. I will walk with the cygnet and barter for way. Surely someone knows where to go, if not I shall guess until it is known."

"Silly, so silly, you are a master of none. There are eyes all upon us, if you're found out, please run." "Run? Why run? I shall walk to my destination. I have committed no crimes upon this dear nation. And if I were to get caught, I will say I am naught, and they'll hear from my heart I am simply lost. Surely this will remedy a cause."

"I wish, oh I wish to be so naive. To live life without worries with my heart on my sleeve. To go to and fro without a care in the world. Wherever you're from, must be a lovely home. Where exactly is it that, so I may know?" Before Willet could respond, there came a vagabond, whistling and spitting and cursing upon. He laughed and he pointed, "Everyone can see your coat. You must lose that apparel if you want to go on."

The girl with the braids grew very afraid. She ran and she ran as fast as she came. She'd never seen a man like that. Wearing such clothes and speaking so frank. She knew what laid underneath, the whispers of nefariousness, a blade in his sheath. For there was not a man like the vagabond in that circle, his voice was more like a witch's cackle.

Willet surprised, grabbed his food, cygnet and raised. The vagabond looked straight in his eyes. "How do you know I want to go on? Is my coat really that obvious, tell me how did you know?" He hissed like a serpent, his bushy mane was all gray, he grinded his teeth as he spoke with his prey.

"I know all there is, that needs to be known. Of crowns and of castles and treasons and their bones. I know of bright coats and I know of dark lairs. You don't belong, says the strings of your hair. But wander around, why should I care?" But it was pretty obvious the vagabond was keen. Willet sized him up, he wasn't what he seemed.

"So then fine fellow, I shall hand you my yellow, you can use it to light your way. I am in no need of it, I just want to exit, if you'll help me, I can be on my way." The gray vagabond looked at his baby swan and he ripped it from his hands. "This shall make due, sliver down to the pools, where the old heroes look over in pride.

There you shall discover clues and signs, and wherever you want to be ye shall find." "Thank you sincerely." "A warning for you, little lamb, little fool. Your coat is not sufficient enough. Not the cygnet or the cider or the pretty braided spider or the bread that crumbles upon your fists can save you.

When you walk, watch your back, anyone could attack, foreign foes blend in like the leaves; Don't forget there's a Queen who will bring you to your knees if you, so make a move that doesn't meet her approval." "Queen you say? Queen Zarday? Or The Queen of Element Skills? There are so many queens, but I shall bow if I see, still." The gray vagabond, in his arms crushed the swan, and his eyes grew larger than giants.

"None of those beings can stand to The Queen and she would have their heads on silver platters. What I really mean, and I hope it is seen, that the highest order is of the eminent SHE." "Eminent SHE? Whatever do you mean? Are you trying to intimidate me?" The gray vagabond vanished right there, Willet looked left then right. He took a deep breath and suddenly realized that this gave him such a fright.

As he went past the pools and the statues of old and new, he noticed darkness clouding the skies. He needed to find a place where he could lay his head, something soft, something cool for a bed. And as he walked, deeper and thicker, mud under his feet, bitter like licorice;

He seemed to be lost in his ever most lost and not a soul to help him out. So he stopped to rest, put his sash on his chest, and his coat would be the warmth, though its brightness could lure animals near he feared.

And in his sleek slumber, he dreamt of the number of pies he could eat in a day. And during that sleep, there was something to see, lurking out yonder. Willet jumped to his feet, yelling "Who is there, let me see!" And glowing red eyes floated side to side. "I see you are bad with directions, you might have missed the intersection, how your immaturity clouds thee." "Who's there? Who are you?" He yelled. Barely visible, he held up his coat.

He could see the outline of a woman of some kind, tousled hair like wispy vines. "I am The Queen, though you see, you've met me, many times on your way to your end. And as impossible as it may seem, I rule all your courses. And abandon is my lesson's key. Though I am made evil by men and their creatures, I hold and possess the greatest features; wisdom at best, see a woman is always put to the test.

But nay today, a man is the victim, he circles his land like a sheep; his innocence threatened but nothing to mention, he's silent when he should speak. You see yourself clever, you've pulled every lever, and my child I am always ahead. If you seek slumber, do not look for lumber, I have a formidable bed."

Willet grew fear and he didn't go near for The Queen seemed potent and strong. He fell to his knees and he said "Please Supreme! Spare my life! I shall not come here again." The Queen got closer, her beauty, her eyes, her fair skin and her thighs. She wore the crown like it was always hers; folklore was nothing compared to before. But underneath the majestic was a demon in question, at least that's what they said.

Every ruby and emerald and jasper and diamond pressed close against her powerful figure. Willet covered his eyes but she grabbed his hands in a surprise and she knelt beside him. "Willet you are a king from Purple Moon and your memory was lost in a great fire.

The ancient ones predicted and the current ones inflicted a forgetful imagery to your sire. And every moment I met with you was one to make you leave. For no king could see mischief and horror and cling to any of these.

And still your kindness was piled upon like honey meets the milk; and every dark was met with light, every sack was silk. And how I longed to tell you the truth, to see if you could really see. And now you have, you've convinced me, that good is where I want to be. For the warriors avenge and tell lies to no end and the tall tales are left to my grimace.

You've accepted me for me, in the darkness in the leaves...that out of nothing there is something, and it can be used to make life!" The Queen's tears fell down and she pressed her face to his skin and put her arm around his shoulder. Willet got up, pushed her to the side and said "Liars are the worst as they get older."

Truly confused, The Queen fell to her side and she looked up at her suitor. "I promise the liars are the ones in the choir, singing praises and then causing blazes. I'm not that monster everyone says I am, I'm much more powerful and important and ..."

"Powerful? Important? You lured me with lies and you sit there explaining like I'll make up my mind. If they said it, it must be true, if they meant it, it's THE TRUTH! You've been a thorn on my side since the moment I've arrived but I thank you for opening my eyes. All you are is a troll and a cry."

"A troll and a cry?" There The Queen rose. To the point where she was over his nose. "A troll and a cry, that's the truest of lies. You saw me as Sesley because a woman applies; applies all her caring, applies all her splendor.

But all of her treasure is when she is tender. From a man you wanted a wish, from a woman a kiss. And as the sea serpent, I swallowed you whole. Because when I want something I let it be known. If a woman does that, she is seen as a monster; If a man does that, he is seen as a father. And in my vagabond, I took the smallest most precious like a man does with his hooks. And you didn't realize I was also the braids and the brook.

She was the one you felt closest to. She was the faith and the pious virtue. A man lives his entire life creating his way for the throne. But a woman's place is always by his side. Even now I fell for that, my my, who would have known?" And in her anger, she grew and grew and her sadness shielded by all that she knew.

And the flames and the rain and the rage had its day and she poured her lashings upon Willet Dime. But small Willet Dime took his sweet little time and he threw his coat over his body. It created an armour and he pulled out asunder what looked like a greatsword. And he slashed to the sky, ripping The Queen from toe to head, her body on the ground.

And as he drew near, she wriggled in fear and he said "That's your place, where you shall always be. I'm not afraid of things that bite, I'm not afraid of things that aren't right, what I am, is afraid of those in my way. Especially if they cause delay. For I am King and you're just a thing. And that's just the way it's always going to be. And I'm the one who will swallow you whole, feed my belly until I get home. And there I will find a Queen to serve me."

And with her bite, Willet felt it worth the smite, and he pressed on until he got home. For what stories you know, aren't always so, and the heroes sometimes have no soul."

CHAPTER TWELVE:

HERE AND NOW

His car rumbled, two children in the backseat, and there I laid thin like a piece of unused cardboard, indestructible and quiet. But I was HERE and it was NOW. Every year he'd come around, laying cheap flowers like many murderers do, thinking their private service is an atonement. He often wondered what could've been, and how I'd look years later and if those children could've been mine.

This time around, he brought them, buckled in; as if they knew anything about what had occurred there many years before. That their merciful hero would never be found out because he was suddenly "born-again" and married and gave the world two offsprings. While he shopped and breathed and watched television shows and golfed and fixed cars and held those kids up, I laid in the same position, in what I thought was FOREVER.

How could he ever be remorseful? What a ridged conundrum and how he tossed that around for a save. Men like Eddie redouble in power while us women stay far behind. Imagine if I was fooled into masculine dictatorship while I was still alive, I'd be a kept wife who's beauty would only serve to cater to his ego and those adolescents in the backseat.

There was clearly a woman pretending to be dull witted, to land herself the definition of a cowboy persona of the 1950's and 60's:

this megalomaniac charmer who no undoubtedly has rearranged her face time and again. Some women say they want it all, but as long as they are under men. "The man is the head of the house" as if she were headless, and were placed on the gold shield of Athena to scare off any other woman from having her man stray.

What I would give to have the ground open wide and swallow all three whole. Imagine that. Never being found. Imagine that. I did imagine it many times. But there were times when Eddie came alone. Unburdened by the image of his children present; kneeling over spaces where I wasn't even under, his guilt eating at him. Kinda. If that were so, maybe he could tell the police what he did and have them dig up my bones and call it a day.

"Eddie The Hero" to serve his culpability. Maybe he wanted me to forgive him. There's that notion. That he was young and naive and is a changed man now. Children always seem to forgive men who are never there but appear years later in their old age, like a twisted repentance. "Maybe if I forgive the sins of my father, I would feel better. After all, he is old and dying."

But a mother is never forgiven for what she's done: she is not quite the martyr like the father. She is dragged across concrete, every secret stripped naked, every mistake brought to light so that the end of her life is almost burning at the stake, engulfing her every memory and forgetting everything she sacrificed herself for. Although this woman has given birth and dedicates her entire life to serve her family, she is easily struck. Books are written against her, wars are waged against her, her body is not really her choice.

She is still very much oppressed, shut up, reduced; when she's raped, it's her fault. When she has a voice, she is too loud or saying too much. When she wants the best for her children, they bite her hand. She is too emotional to be a leader, too strong to be independent. She doesn't laugh enough, she's too serious, she's problematic, she's not ready.

NO LAWS ARE EVER IN HER FAVOR. But a man is so quickly forgiven. He might not have had enough love; he might have been provoked to be who he has become. The shell of a man does not limit him. His maniacal schemes are often what gets him in positions of power. His emotional outcries often lead to women losing their heads, literally.

His good looks could crack a whip, where his mythology is gospel. A god was absolute while a goddess could die even if she has immortality. Crowds of men lead petulant wars, while crowds of women design standards and ask for some scrap of equality.

A man writes a book or paints a masterpiece and it is wholly marveled. A woman writes a book or paints a masterpiece and she is a recluse; some old maid who never found her suitor. Eddie could lead a regime and half a country would follow him; I could lead with love and be lucky if someone saw me walking down the street. Now would be the time to appear to him. To say "Hello Eddie, remember me?" A reminder to why he comes down every year to "visit."

Getting back in his car, he took his gloves off, looking in the rear view mirror. His little girl combed her doll, the boy writing on the frosted window. I could end it all. See his car ignite in flames, watching steadily as the horror becomes mere whispers. Like my screams had no say in any matter. He knew my demise and perhaps it was sweet karma to die this way in certainty. But he could never handle death like I do.

But I could see a little finger writing slowly on the window's frost. It was my name: J A C I N D A. His son then rolled down his window and looked directly at me, his smile as sweet as fresh cut oranges.

Rolling his window back up, he waved as his father drove off.

****

"Do me a favor and turn off the news please!" Josie yelled from the bed. "I can't stand seeing him talk. It's outrageous that people believe that nonsense!" "Some people really like him. They want this country back to how it was." "Dennis, what does that even mean? Back to how it was? Segregated? Burning crosses? I don't think so!"

"Why do you always have to do that Josie? Always have to make a mockery outta everything I say. Just doesn't make much sense." "What doesn't make much sense is this President. That campaign and those people behind it! It's so preposterous and everyone can see past that charlatan." "He's a very fine actor I'll have you know!"

"Fine actor? Really? What have you seen from Ronald Reagan that is fine? Please name one film. I'll wait." "Dark Victory was pretty good..." "Bette Davis carried that one. Name another." "Okay, well he was pretty good in Bedtime For Bonzo. I watched that film on reruns every Saturday night as a kid."

"The chimp movie? Oh be serious Dennis. You're starting to sound your age." "Well he's an older gentleman so what movie am I supposed to summon up? The Exorcist or somethin'?" "What in God's green earth would make you think of The Exorcist, of all films?" "I dunno. You always put me on the spot. You always have something negative to say about everything!" "About everything? Like...everything? Wow, nice way to round up what this marriage is all about pal."

"You know very well what I mean Josie. You have to debunk and you have to argue and you have to find a bad thing in everything. I suppose it's just in your nature." "Well, you're part of my everything, so I suppose that's a bad thing? Or do you just mean that I can't stand injustice? Or when Republicans stand on their BS morality soapbox spewing nonsense to The American People?

You remember when we ate at Lum's on vacation and those people were wearing those stupid pins and talking loudly so everyone could hear their conversation? Spewing BS about jobs and living near Afro-Americans?" "They were just saying how they had to move out cuz' the neighborhoods were getting bad. But we didn't live in that area so I wasn't very pressed to understand what they meant."

"Looks like ya know exactly what they meant! I'm sure you feel that way around here, now that we've settled in and bought this house, huh?" "I'm not racist Josie. I've never been racist. Just because I don't like the loud music doesn't make me a racist. And I resent you for implying that. I really do. Maybe I should go downstairs and watch sports and leave you to your mechanisms."

"So quick to skedaddle when I'm pointing out the facts, huh? I know you're not a racist sweetheart but sometimes you say things that make me wonder." "Make you wonder about what, Josie? I'm as Conservative as butter, and you've always known that. I moved here for you. You liked this area and you wanted to be around your family. So we're here cuz' I love you. Right?"

Josie laughed. "Okay wait a minute...we have to talk about this." "About what?" "Conservative as butter? Where in God's name did you come up with that? When has butter been Conservative?" "It's a saying is all." "A saying?" Josie made her way out of the bed, pushing the covers down with her feet. She wobbled over to where Dennis was sitting.

"You're gonna make me have this baby right here on this floor, I swear! I don't think I've ever heard anything so funny in my life.

Conservative as butter? Is that cuz' Farmers are supposedly Conservative and they milk cows and churn and all that mess? Does that make the butter Conservative?" "I guess so." Josie covered her mouth.

"That is about the silliest saying that I've ever heard in my life! It's right up there with 'The chickens are coming home to roost.'" Josie let out a big chuckle and Dennis rolled his eyes. "You sure are a beautiful mean girl, you know that?" Josie put her arms around Dennis and kissed him. "I'm just teasin' you Dennis. You'd think we grew up in two different areas, but you lived right down the street! You're so cute!" "Yeah, yeah yeah! Conservative as butter is the right phrase." "I think you mean Conservative and All-American as apple pie. Not butter silly!"

"If you weren't so pregnant, I'd climb you Josie." Dennis ran his fingers through Josie's hair and she struggled to sit on his lap. "What's stopping you? Dennis I want you to know that you married a strong, intelligent and capable woman. Someone who makes her own decisions and doesn't back down. You knew that. That's what made you chase after me. That and my supple breasts of course!"

"You do have some pretty breasts. Especially now, since they're so big." "They're big but so is my brain. And if you think I'm gonna walk around letting my husband think he's going to stay a Republican, you have another thing coming." "I don't consider myself anything!

Shoot, I hardly vote! I was just brought up in a certain kind of way and that's my life. And I respect that, so you should too." "I can't respect oppression and the minimizing of other people. Or painting others that don't look like us in a negative light. I don't respect that and I won't stand for it. That's a deal-breaker."

"Woman, the deed is done! That ring around your finger was the deal-breaker. We're married and that's life. I get that you have feminist liberal views and I have my staunch Right leanings. Oh well. Get over it." "My sister had an abortion." "Your sister?" "Yes! My sister. She's dead but it doesn't mean she never existed. Jacinda?"

"I know baby. I just didn't know she had an abortion." "She'd gotten pregnant and my mother wasn't having it. She made her get an abortion." "Oh wow. I'm sorry to hear that." "Well, I'm not. The circumstances were different. In 1975, parents had a say, especially us girls who were under lock and key. My mother is overprotective as you know."

"Well, it's too late to get one now!" Dennis joked. Josie got up and walked towards the window. "In all seriousness Dennis...if I made a decision not to have this kid...you know...in the beginning..." "You don't want our baby?" "I'm not saying that! Of course I want her. I'm just saying that, what if...what if I would've come to you and said 'I'm not ready to have this baby.' Would you understand?"

"Absolutely not. I'd never terminate my child!" "OUR child Dennis." "Well that's what I meant!" "Okay, well what if it was on the table. Would you have considered it? If I gave you some valid reasons?" "No. I told you. Absolutely not. It's my first born and also, we're married and I'm as ready as you. We both have great jobs and we have a home for her. So my answer is NO."

"What if I was raped?" "What?!" "Raped Dennis. Remember that movie we saw where the woman gets raped by some perpetrator and she has to live with the trauma?" "What movie was that?" "That movie we watched last Sunday." "Which one?" "Focus, Dennis for crying out loud! What if...that happened to me?"

"I'd kill the son of a bitch! I'd hunt him down and kill him!" "Right, but that's not the point." "It is to me. Ain't no man gonna rape my wife and get away with it!" "This is why I can't have conversations with you Dennis." "Well what do you want me to say Josie? That a rape means it's okay to kill a life? That I'm gonna come home and comfort you after a rape and say 'okay so we're gonna kill it?' No way! I'm not a murderer."

"So we'd raise another man's child? Someone we don't know, that raped me and could possibly still be out there?" "You're making me nervous Josie. Are you trying to tell me something? Is there someone out there who..." "No! No...I'm just trying to give you a worst case scenario. Because I believe that a woman has a choice and the right to choose. And yes, the husband also has that choice, clearly.

But there are so many women who aren't ready to have children, who get raped. Whoever...whatever circumstance it is, have that option." "Roe vs. Wade I get it." "Do you though? Because it's not just about some law or The Supreme Court. It's about men dictating the bodies of women."

"I got it. I do. I know it seems like I'm some schlep from outer space, but I get your point. I just wasn't raised to think that way." "The point is, neither was I Dennis. My mother made a decision for my sister that was my sister's to make. And that's fucked up, you know? Jacinda should've had a say in it. But my mother acted out of fear and her version of love. She thought it was the only solution to that problem."

"You miss your sister huh?" "I don't wanna talk about that. That's too much for me to handle." "I get it. I just thought it would be nice to ask you. You hardly talk about her. And when you do, you're standoffish." "I talk about her." "Yeah, when it's about a news article or something you see on TV that reminds you of her. But you don't really talk about her. I'm surprised you told me about her tonight."

"I much rather would talk about Bedtime For Bonzo." "Hey don't knock it! It was a 'nature vs. nurture' movie. Pretty fun and educational. We loved that film." "That 'nature vs. nurture' shit were experiments on babies. I saw the videos in school and it's disgusting. Who could do such a thing?" "It's Psychology babe." "Oh? That's okay but abortion isn't? You might be a bit liberal after all!" "Yeah you wish!"

****

Josie gave birth to her first child. The blanket swept delicately in a tuck, she stared into the eyes of her daughter. The sterile nurses' outfits coming in and out in shifts, the breasts leaking, out for the child to suckle. Dennis's empty coffee cups and half read novel on the chair. The moments passing in anticipation like trains in the night and every much of it was worth it to watch her sleep.

In a wheelchair and then into the minivan; Josie watched it all unfold as she took in the winter air mixed with forced heat. She sat day after day, her baby nestled under her bosom, running her finger along her tiny nose. "You look just like your aunt Jaci." The smell of banana pancakes in the house, fried eggs and salted ham turned into bits of cereal on the floor, the blaring sound of cartoons and the enigmatic emptiness crippling inside.

"You're not sleeping enough." Her mother said. Josie shrugged and tried to piece together a unicorn puzzle with her 2 year-old daughter. "I'm thinking about planning a trip to Bermuda if you'd like to come with me honey." "Mom...Mom I cannot focus, I'm trying to find a piece to this puzzle. What made Dennis buy such a complicated puzzle for a toddler?"

"Did you hear me Josie? It would be so nice if we could take a cruise like we did when you girls were younger." "We didn't take a cruise mom." "Sure we did! Don't you remember?" "No Mom. That was you, Herman and I. Jacinda wasn't there. It was AFTER." "Well that's what I meant." "No, you didn't! You said when 'us girls were younger.' Jacinda was seventeen when she disappeared so we never went on any cruises with her."

"The point is...sweetheart...that I'd like to see you relax again. It would be nice if we could spend some time together. That's all." "I have a toddler now. I mean...I have a lot on my plate with work and commitments and Dennis and his Lupus. We have our hands full." "Oh, okay. Well then maybe in the Summer? We can take Jackie and it would be so nice!"

"Mom...I'm just trying to get situated. I'm exhausted. I think we have a leak in the basement and I still haven't called someone for it. I'm just...so...tired." Josie shifted in her chair and patted her mother's hand. "Tell you what? If we have some time, We'll take a trip to the beach or something. It'll be with all of us. That would be nice." "Can I ask you something without you getting mad at me hun?"

"Of course Mom." "Well put your puzzle piece down I'm trying to have a conversation with you!" "What do you want from me?!" "Fine! Fine! I'll just get my purse and come back when you're not in one of your moods." "What do you mean 'one of my moods?'"

"You know exactly what I mean and I'm not gonna say it in front of Dennis or the baby." "Go ahead, I'm listening. Cuz' you know...I've just been really tired. Having children is a lot of work." "Oh really?! Tell me about it! I had two!" "It doesn't seem like it sometimes Mom..." "What is that supposed to mean Josie?" "IT MEANS...it... means that it's a lot of work...for me."

"No, that was a dig! That was definitely a dig! How am I supposed to feel, Queen Josie? Huh? Am I supposed to like, feel sorry for myself like you do? Cry all the time? Be miserable with my life? Ding ding ding! I already did that! It never goes away Josie. You know? It never goes away!"

"Well you moved on pretty quickly it seems." "Yeah?" "Yes MOTHER! You met Herman soon after, you ignored me for a while. It was like...like Jaci never existed." "How could you say that? How was I supposed to feel, Josie? Huh? You think losing a child is easy? That it all has to be put on display so people can see I am grieving? I'm not a showboat Josie!"

Josie pushed her hands across the puzzle and threw it all to the floor. She was subsumed with pain and anger. "OH HOW I WISH YOU UNDERSTOOD THE PAIN!" She screamed. Dennis ran into the dining room and grabbed Jackie.

"I understand pain Josie! I understand completely..." "THEN WHY DID YOU SAY YOU LOST A CHILD??? HUH!? SHE WAS NEVER FOUND! YOU GAVE UP ON HER! YOU GAVE UP! YOU GAVE UP ON US!!" "Gave up?" Dennis put Jackie in her playpen and put his hands on Josie's shoulders but she shrugged them off. "You can't keep walking into this place expecting me to not be broken Mom! You are good at pretending but I am not!"

"No one's pretending here Josie Lynn! Not for a moment! I didn't know how to cope! I didn't know how to make sense of it all. One day she's at the pool with you, and the next I'm filing police reports and putting signs up. It's not easy. I tried...I tried to throw myself out of the window of the funeral home, did you know that?" "No..."

"WELL I DID! To have everyone there gather, to an empty casket! To stand outside in that...cemetery...knowing she could be out there, alive...probably held against her will. It is something a mother never gets over. Never forgets Josie. I will never forget. I remember on birthdays especially...on Mother's Day when I don't see her around. I could've had something to remember her by as a child. But even that...was my fault."

Josie walked over to her mother and wrapped her arms around her. She gently kissed her face and wiped her tears. She pressed her head against her mother's and whispered, "That's all I wanna hear sometimes Mommy. That she's not gone. That she's always here with us."

"She is, baby. Who can forget that beautiful spirit? She'll never go away. Don't ever think I forgot. Please don't ever do that or say that again!" "I know...I won't. I'm sorry. Ever since I had Jackie...I just don't feel like myself. Just been so tired. It's like something took over me. Can't focus or clean or do anything."

"I'll go to the doctor with you if you want? Maybe something is wrong." "I think so Mommy." "Oh baby. I'm so sorry. I didn't know you had all those feelings bottled up inside. I much would have preferred a different setting." Josie laughed and kissed her mother. "You want some coffee?" "I think this calls for some. Do you plan on making any dinner? Dennis looks hungry."

"I'm not saying anything." Dennis joked. "Mom?" "Yes baby?" "I'm sorry I doubted you." "You didn't doubt me. I should be more open and honest." "Yeah...me too." "We'll know the truth one day." "I know."

CHAPTER THIRTEEN:

THE DARK ROOM

"Can you hear me spirit? If you're there, make your presence known."

Violently jolting, Blaire lifted her arms trying to grab onto anything. Her nerve endings tactile and acute, fleshing out formations of fingers with every increased friction. Her nails dug into the front and side of a table. "I'm here." "Spirit?" "I'M HERE."

Umezda's palms began to sweat. This was his first time having a seance and he wasn't entirely sure it was going to work. He had his royal purple curtains up, a grand oak table that he got at a second hand shop and a lace table covering he bought online that was supposed to look vintage. He knew he had a gift, but this was the first time he was putting it to use in a grandiose way.

"Okay so she says she's here. She's definitely here. Do you want to say something to her?" Josie had seen several of these things play out on television and she had always wondered what it would be like, but now that she was sitting there, across from three other strangers, she was starting to have second thoughts. "How do you know it's her? Can you ask her if she's my sister...or...her name? Please?"

Umezda placed both of his hands flat on the table, shuffling in his chair. He'd gotten contact, as miraculous as that was for him, but he was afraid the presence would scatter or fade away. He lowered his head, closed his eyes and concentrated turning over one hand. "Spirit if you are still here, what is your name?"

Umezda was sure nothing would come of it, but surely there was a glow by the window and a silhouette of an appearance. He was the first to notice, but he didn't want to freak the other clients out so he closed his eyes. "What is your name?" He repeated. The spirit transfigured from a silent intangible glow to a young woman afraid to move forward. The figure pressed her face against the purple curtains.

Suddenly, the curtains caught fire and the clients began to scream, fumbling out of their places. "Please everyone calm down!" Umezda ran into the kitchen, pouring a glass of water and putting out the fire. He felt panic-stricken, a pain in the pit of his stomach churning away. But he knew he needed to reassure his clients that everything was okay.

"Ladies please have a seat. Take your places please!" His hands fluttering towards the chairs. "There's no need to be alarmed. Spirits often make a mark or leave a sign. They want to prove that they are present and aware that we know they are present. In this instance, it is only one..." "That you're aware of!" Anette yelled. "That I'm aware of, yes!

You're absolutely right! But you see, spirits are like us, wandering this earth, not jaunting about but trying to find answers. Proving themselves is nothing they HAVE to do, but choose to. And that's great in our instance. We must make them feel welcomed. They must be free from threat or danger."

"I just wanted to know if my sister Jacinda would make contact.

I should've agreed to do a one on one and not be so cheap. I think this was a mistake." Leah was the only one in her seat. She was still and had her eyes closed, her hands overlapping one another. Anette slowly moved towards her. "Hey Leah are you okay?" Leah moved her head to the left as if permuting what she was feeling, and then down again. Umezda knew this wasn't normal. "Please let's take our seats.."

"I am here." Leah said. Her voice striking and pronounced, her eyes lucid and outstretched. Josie and Anette watchfully sat down and fixed their glaze to Leah. "Blaire." Umezda wiped his forehead, pushing his chair forward towards Leah. "No one makes a sound please. She's making contact and...and she's using Leah as a vessel. 'Your name...it's Blaire?'"

"Blaire. Yes. My name is...Blaire." "Hello Blaire. Welcome to this meeting. Please tell us where you come from?" "Come from?" "Yes." Umezda could feel his left leg trembling, but tried to control it. His knees were shaking nervously and his face was sweltering. "Where do you come from?" "I'm...ah....I don't really know." "Okay...okay, so...how did you pass?" Blaire raised her hands and slowly placed them on the back of her head. She could hear the gunshots again.

It took her a minute to respond but the events were extremely vivid in her mind. "I was murdered. I was killed. But I don't know where I went. Where am I now?" "2010." Anette whispered. She looked over at Umezda with tears in her eyes. "Excuse me Umezda but do you mind me speaking to Blaire for one moment?"

"Oh? Yes, of course. Just simple questions, nothing to overwhelm or trouble her." "Okay. 'Blaire, were you the woman who was murdered along with her kids in 1991? I'd like to know.'"
Blaire felt as if she had cotton-mouth, her tongue felt swollen and arrid. She grabbed the glass sitting on the table but there was no

water left. "If he gets me a glass of water to sip on, I'll gladly tell you."

Umezda shot up, hoping she would be querulous after the drink, scurrying to the kitchen, pouring the water. "Shit." He thought. "What did I get myself into? I'm not doing this anymore. Jeez. This is getting out of hand. Is she pretending? She can't be. Maybe she is! Some people like attention. But maybe she isn't. We'll see. I'm gonna have to test her."

Umezda slowly settled the glass of water in front of Leah and sat down. Leah picked up the glass and took a sip. "Thank you. It feels like an eternity without tasting it. Yes!" "Yes?" "Umezda asked. "Yes to her question." Pointing at Anette, she continued. "I am the woman who was murdered. HE TOOK MY BABIES!" Leah lifted the table, still possessed by Blaire, hurling it across the room. Everyone was pushed down to the floor like magnets. Umezda tried to get up but couldn't.

Leah stood there with her eyes colorless, her hair went from brown to white. Her body was suspended in the air, her fingertips voltaic like balls of fire. Water began to spew from her mouth and then she dropped to the floor languorously.

She closed her eyes and stumbled towards Josie. "What happened?" Josie piled out of her pull and grabbed Leah who was feeling weak. "It's okay sweetie. You were being used...by a spirit." "What? A spirit? Oh my God! What?! I think I want to get out of here!" Umezda pulled open the curtains and led the women into his kitchen.

"Okay ladies it's time for real talk. I've seen things before, but this one is kind of scaring the shit out of me. I know I'm supposed to be your spirit guide and all that bullshit, but this was some kind of intense stuff. I mean, am I the only one here that feels this way?"

Leah shook her head and said, "I wanted to see if my auntie Rosalind, who was murdered by that serial killer in Chicago would come through but instead I became some pawn for this evil spirit." Josie interjected, "I don't think she was evil."

"I agree." Anette joined. "I know her. Kinda. Blaire was killed by my uncle. He was unstable. My grandmother didn't want anything to do with him because he was so sick. Mental health runs in the family and he ended up murdering his wife and kids. It's so sad. It's kind of sweet that she decided to show up for me."

Umezda thought, "Yeah, but what if she wanted to kill you?" Then Josie blurted out, "What if she wanted to kill you? You know, for being related to him? I mean, I doubt that. But it might be kind of weird for her to know. I'm not sure how ghosts accept time and how it is over there on the other side.

I'm only saying that because it must be so sad to lose your children like that. And to lose your life too. I have four grown daughters and it would absolutely kill me if a man did that to them. Even though I'm pretty sure it was done to my sister."

"Please don't tell me anymore about that. I prefer the spirits communica..." "Oh, I think the spirits communicated alright. You girls are pretty young but I'm a bit older, so maybe I should advise you to be careful."

Umezda put on a pot of coffee. "Listen, for a long time, I've been dealing with this gift. I call it a gift because it is extremely delicate and important. It's important because my job is to help people and I'm helping all of you. To contact your loved ones and to make sure we send them to the light, even though I'm not exactly sure if that's what happens or what I believe. I don't even know if that's what I'm supposed to say, but I'm saying it. Does that make sense?"

"Sorta. How old were you when all of this came to you? Your gift?" Anette asked. "To be quite honest, I'm not sure. It's just been there, lingering. I was raised in an evangelical church, so they teach you to suppress it and to believe that all of that is evil. And while I've seen some true evil in that church, this is something else. Something totally different and exceptional.

From what I saw today, it might be. But she didn't seem evil. She looked like a grieving mother. I'm not mad at her for burning my curtain. It's from 'Cornie's' so I knew that polyester was gonna go somehow." They all laughed in unison. Umezda placed chunks of chocolate biscotti in front of each of them.

"You ladies seem like you're all connected extraordinarily in some way or another. It's always interesting to see people interact with each other under these kinds of circumstances. But I noticed you three worked well during this seance. Thank you for that. Now I'm not saying to hurry up and become The Charmed Ones, but it's nice to see that kind of Girl Power."

Josie smiled and applied some mauve lipstick. "It's too bad this color is discontinued. And if I ask for it online, I'm afraid I might get trolled because the guy who makes it is a pretty terrible human being. But it's the only pigment that I love." She passed the tube of lipstick around. Leah laughed.

"You're talking about Lyle 'The Lips' Quinn. So problematic. Lord! So problematic! I mean, what in your right mind would make you use all kinds of racist epithets and then turn around and think people were not going to find out? Social Media doesn't fuck around! That color is so good though."

Crunching into his biscotti, Umezda interjected. "Everything good? There's cream right there." Anette nodded and asked, "Hey Umezda, I have a quick question: So, now that Leah has been possessed by a spirit, does that mean it'll follow her home and haunt her family and friends? Not trying to be creepy but is that even a possibility?" "Oh girl please do not say that! I have enough problems with my ex and clingy mom." Leah replied.

Umezda laughed. "I don't think Blaire came through to haunt anyone. I think she's lost. She wasn't even sure where she came from. It's a possibility that if she was going to be anywhere, it would be here...with us. And Anette, I'll make sure your family gets closure. I know this is a wild find and such an experience. I also wanna thank Leah for being a brave soldier and letting Blaire come through."

"I don't think I had any other choice!" Leah quipped. "How did it feel?" Anette asked. "I dunno. I can't really remember it. I know there was the whole curtains burning situation and then suddenly I was standing there and the table was tossed over. My hands are a little sore but I'm okay." Umezda opened his cupboard, pulled out two small towels and ran it under warm water.

He placed it around Leah's wrists. "There you go Leah. I hope it feels better." "Thank you Umezda. Where did that name come from? Or is it some psychic hocus pocus name that you made up?" "Sadly, this is my name. And short answer: Yes."

Josie's phone began to vibrate in her pocket. "Excuse me one second everyone, I have to take this...it's my daughter Jackie. 'Hey babe, what's up? Yes...I'm gonna be home in a bit. I was just out grabbing some groceries. Yes. Okay fine, I was at a seance...yes... yeah girl in the daytime...I'll talk to you in a bit. Where's my granddaughter? Okay, good. Love you. Bye.'

Sorry. That was my eldest Jackie. It would've been nice to share the information of being in contact with my sister. I was sooo looking forward to it." "What happened to her?" Leah asked. "She disappeared in '76. We were very close. Sometimes it's hard to remember because it was almost 35 years ago and the case went cold.

It's extremely frustrating to talk about it, but it's the only way to keep her memory alive. My mother passed in 2003, I'll be 51 in September and I just want to know what happened to her." Leah sipped her coffee and put her hand on Josie's. "Awe, I know it hurts. Wow. I can't imagine losing my sister. What did the police say?" "The police didn't have much of a lead. There was the jealous jaded boyfriend and the town kind of knows it was him.

I mean, it's obvious. He left, but only three towns over. The guy changed his name, all of the usual suspect stuff. And the cops loved him because he was connected with them. I think one of his cousins still works there, so my sister was never found. I was the only eye witness.

I saw her leave with him, and then she vanished. It's a lot of pain, I won't lie. It is a lot. Because she was plucked away from us. So young. So beautiful. I wanted to be her. She was the sweetest sister anyone could ever ask for. Then she was gone in an instant.

I've been approached by these shows to get her name out there but I don't want my kids and grandkids dragged into all of it. My oldest daughter Jackie tried being an amateur sleuth but it just never panned out. You know? Talking about panning out, I gotta jet. Gotta grab some food and then to Jackie's.

It was quite an experience ladies. I hope you all find peace and what you're looking for." Umezda walked Josie out and gave her a hug. "If you'd like, I'd love for you to come back alone. You can bring your daughters, but alone would be better. I think we could contact Jacinda and get to the bottom of it. What do you think?"

"I don't know. I'd have to really be up for it. All of this shook me up. I think it would be nice but hopefully she's not into burning anything or tossing tables, though I wouldn't blame her at this point." "Me neither! You're a sweet lady Josie. You have my card. Think about it." "I will. Thank you Umezda." "My pleasure."

CHAPTER FOURTEEN:

SCARLET FEVER

Ellen scanned each product and then the coupons. She hated when they came in with coupons. Always expired and always in the mood to argue. She knew the business of disgruntled customers so she always pretended to scan the old coupons and then manually give them a discount. It was already a mom and pop shop and she didn't want her repeat customers to go to The Home Depot down the highway.

She gave her nephew Scooby a dirty stare and then grabbed a packet of gum, throwing it his direction. "Please put those nails in the order they're supposed to go cuz' you've been slacking for a week! That girl better not come up in here when you're working! And why doesn't your mother pick up the phone? She got worms for brains?"

"She's at Sally's. She's getting her dress sewn up. It ripped when she was at the theater." "Yeah, I bet. Lemme guess…near the knees?" "Awe auntie you sure have a mind for filth! Keep my momma's name clean." "Alright then kid, alright. Just joking. She's my sister. If Irene doesn't mind, you shouldn't. I'll say jokes if I wanna. Where's your uncle Tyson?"

"He's in the back filing up some papers." "Oh? Well man the ship while I have a few words with him." "Yes ma'am!" "Good boy." Ellen made her way to the back and turned the knob. It was locked. She banged on the door and said, "Tyson Rufus Brandt open the fucking door this instant! Why is it locked?" Tyson fumbled slowly to the door and unlocked it.

"Old woman it was unlocked." "Don't bullshit me Tyson, what's the door locked for? We got some accountant calling again? You need me to call Scooby? He got good eyesight, he could write up some of those numbers for you." "Old woman leave me be! I'm just making some phone calls." "About?" Ellen pulled up one of the suede chairs and plopped herself into it. "About?" "Cool your jets, it's just Jesse and them tryin' to sell those candles again. You know... the maple ones don't nobody like?"

"You didn't lock the damn door for some candles Ty, now quit playing games and tell me what's wrong. We got money missing? Cuz' I lent Scoob some green for his prom tuxedo. You know I don't like him lookin' poor when he got us." "I know. It ain't no money, though you can be a lot nicer and stop scaring off these customers." "It's called old age Tyson." "It's called being a grouch all the damn time like people owe you something! You got menopause now. You're an old broad, so start acting like it. Just try and be nice.

Mrs. Toronto keeps coming in, hiding behind the aisles tellin' Scooby you got some stick up your ass." "That old windbag shitting on me? Didn't she steal a few corn cans at the supermarket and blamed the Hispanic kid even though they have footage of her stealing? Old bat." "C'mon mother we're barely making ends meet. I wanna leave this door banger to Harvey one day."

"I know! I know! I'll adjust my 'tude!' Where is Harvey?" "Close that door. Lock it." Ellen flung the door shut and clicked the lock. "I swear to them saints if you tell me Harvey is in some kind of trouble again..." "Shhh SHHH! Shut up, you know Scoob always has his nosy ears pressed up against everything. Don't want his chatty mom telling the entire town about Harvey."

"Why not? He sure deserves it with what he's put us through. He's your son Tyson! I love em' and all, he's my sweetheart but I got that handful while your last old maid had the sense to up and leave to Chillicothe." "You would think you're his mom with how ungrateful you are." "I'm just kidding. You know my sense of humor, don't act brand new Tyson."

"Well I just hung up with Harvey. And Ellen it's real bad. I don't think we can smooth this one over." "Whatcha mean?" "He's over in....is that damn door locked?" "Yes! He's over in where?" "Ellen I'm really scared for that boy. I really am!" "Tyson you're scaring me." "He's in Oregon." "Oregon? Oregon? What's he doing all the way up there?"

"Sheriff Hurley and I had a talk and it's not looking too good." "Okay then fix it. You know Sheriff Hurley! Get him to turn the other way! How much is he asking for now?" "That's just it Ellen. He's telling me that I need to sell the store AND the house and leave. That's what he said." "Sell the...what? Wait what? What does he mean? We're not leaving!"

"Ellen you gotta hush up and listen! And stop talking so damn loud, woman! You sound like an alarm clock! I don't want this to get out. Not Sally, not Scoob, not Carson...nobody needs to know. Not yet." "But I'm confused Tyson. We've lived here all our lives. This is where we belong, right? I'm not leaving. What does he mean?"

"Ellen you're just not getting it in the noggin." Tyson lowered his head sullen. "Well calm down! Why are you breaking into tears for? What's really going on?" "Ellen, I really need you to stop the bullshit and this coddling bit!" "I beg your pardon?" "You wanna go to jail too?" "Jail?!" "Ellen, stop acting so damn surprised.

I told you to stop enabling this boy...man....he needs to figure out his shit. But you said, 'that's your boy.'" "Well he is! He's our boy. I'm not gonna let Harvey go to jail. That's our son!" "Well then you talk to Sheriff Hurley because he's saying that Harvey is looking at life, no parole! At least that's what it's looking like." "Life with no parole? Not Harvey! Can't we offer them some money?" "This ain't no damn house auction Ellen! Dammit listen to me! Harvey went off and killed another damn girl! You know this is beyond us! He got them crazy genes! He's got issues."

"He didn't do any of those things!" "Holy shit! You're crazier than him Ellen. You really are! I'm not afraid to wrap my mouth down a barrel of a gun cuz' I'm already an old eagle. I'll shoot square through my skull, I don't give a fuck!" "Stop it Tyson, you're talking nonsense!" "Woman you better repent of your sins, you better be ready. Cuz' God is gonna get us good!"

"Stop all that holy roller nonsense! We gotta come up with a plan. Maybe...maybe we do sell this god forsaken shit store and that house. We just put in another room so we can get a pretty penny for it. And we can join Harvey..." "Harvey? Harvey is gonna be in jail you stupid bitch! He's in Oregon on his own. We're going to Florida. Sooner or later they'll find his son of a bitch ass and jail em' but we're gonna be in Daytona with the sun. I'm too old for this shit."

"I thought you said you were gonna shoot that old head off of yours! Now you're in Daytona? Make some sense old fool." "Ellen, we gotta wash our hands with Harvey." "I can't do that Tyson. I...I really can't. That's my boy. I ain't give birth to him but he's my son. He's had a hard life." "Hard life? He's a privileged piece of shit who took advantage of our kindness. That's what he is! Get your head out of the clouds and let's focus."

"I'm focused. What's your plan, old fool?" "I say we sell the store, the house, cement that basement floors, make sure nobody digs there. Sell the house to your sister if you want. I got plenty of money put away and some more at John John's. If Irene got that old house, she won't let anyone dig. And if they do, we'll be dead by then."

"Alright. Alright! Sounds like this is what we're forced to do. What if Sheriff Hurley rats us out?" "He said he won't. He said he won't go after Harvey if he can stop it. But he says the state might intervene and he doesn't wanna lose his job. You know he shot that kid a few years back. He can't have that bite him in the ass."

"Does that mean that Harvey might get caught?" "Yes mother. Yes that's exactly what that means. Haven't you been listening to a word I said? We gotta let him go! We say that we didn't know, okay? We'll move to Daytona..." "Why Daytona? Why not Miami or Orlando?" "Focus!" "I'm focused. I just don't like car racing. Why can't we move near an amusement park or Ocean Drive? Why do it gotta be near them cars that race around? Daytona? Tyson we got the money. What else is in Daytona?"

"I can't believe you're worried about Daytona and not us going to jail. Cuz' that's a possibility too!" "Well, we ain't do nothin' so..." "What the fuck do you mean we didn't do nothin?? Are you out of your fucking mind? We helped him bury those two whores. And we helped him dump that boy...that boy from..."

"Stop! Don't say his name. It's so sad. He didn't mean to...he didn't mean to! You said it yourself that he got problems." "He shot em' six times Ellen! Face the damn music. Your son is a serial killer. He got people missing everywhere! We've seen those signs go up and like dummies we have to volunteer to help look for the bodies. I, for one, am glad that'll be over. And for the record, Harvey was obsessed with that boy."

"He wasn't obsessed…" "He was twelve! A damn pedophile is what he is! Stalking that boy all over the place til' he had his way with him." "I can't believe you're saying that here! Scooby is right outside that door! If he hears any of this, we are done for!" "Scoob won't sing. Unless he wants Harvey to do something about it." "Well old fool, when do we start all of this? And isn't it a bit suspicious that we just up and leave?"

"Sheriff Hurley says that it's the best idea for now and it'll rule us out. I trust him so we gotta start doing all the transactions. I know a few people who owe me money and I'll link up with you at home. Please take all of this seriously mother. Please, and don't call Harvey." "Well, I don't have his number!" "Don't answer his phone calls either."

"So this is it Tyson? I gotta let go of my son? Just like that?" "I mean…it's the best we can do Ellen. Until it all smooths over. Alright go out there and start cleaning up. I'm gonna make some more phone calls." "Okay. Okay. Okay, I said! Okay…" Ellen closed the door behind her and made her way towards the register.

"Hey auntie? I got a hold of my momma. She's home now, if you wanna give her a ring." "Why would I wanna call her?!" She snapped. "Didn't you say you were looking for her?" "Oh..yeah… okay Scooby. Thank you doll. I'll give her a ring. You can start cleaning up, we're closing early." "Oh? Okay." "Hey Scooby?" "Yeah auntie Ellen?" "Your girlfriend…what's her name?"

"Julie?" "Yeah….Julie. She's real nice. She's good for you." "Thanks auntie. I like her a lot." "That's sweet, nephew. Go on and clean up and dust off those shelves up top. I can't reach. Your auntie is getting old and she's getting shorter." "Will do auntie. No worries!"

Ellen dug into her nails, gnawing them off one by one. She went to the door to lock it, but someone pulled at the handle. "We're closed darlin' but tomorrow we're open bright and early." "It'll be quick, I just need some sharp-nose pliers. It'll only take a second." Ellen thought about what Tyson said about her behavior lately towards customers so she said "Come right in. But make it quick darlin' we wanna get out of here soon."

"Thank you ma'am, I sure will. What aisle?" Scooby showed the woman where the pliers were and the woman placed the pliers in front of Ellen. "Okay! Those are some great pliers for jewelry making. Great if your husband is an Electrician. There are some cheaper ones towards the back. Hey Scoob, please show this young lady to the cheaper pliers, I'm sure she's not trying to empty her bank on these."

"Sure thing auntie!" "These will do just fine." "Okay! Never mind Scooby she wants these!" "Okay!" Scooby echoed. The woman watched as Ellen scanned the pliers. "That'll be 6.50." The woman slowly reached into her purse and pulled out a bag of coins. Ellen tried to hide her disdain but she rolled her eyes anyway.

"I'm sorry ma'am..I just have these quarters, just give me a second." "It's quite alright sweety, it's legal tender. Take your time, just not too much time cuz' like I said we're.." Scooby ducked his head out and smiled at Ellen but Ellen was not amused. "...Tryin' to get out early. Need help with that sweety?" "No, I'm fine. I'm just counting them in my head. I was at four dollars but I lost count. Forgive me."

"It's alright darlin' I lose count all the time." "Thank you." Ellen felt her palms begin to sweat. She was soaking her armpits. She wanted the woman to pay and leave already but she was trying to take heed of Tyson's advice. But the woman was testing her patience.

She stood there eye-balling the young lady, tapping her fingers on the cash register.

"Got your counting together yet?" "Do you mind not interrupting me, I'm trying to count. This is the second time already." Ellen put her hands up and motioned a zipped lip. She looked over at Scooby and grinned from ear to ear. The woman placed the quarters on the counter and let out a loud sneeze. "God bless you!" Ellen quipped.

"How do you know that?" "Uh, know what sweety?" "That God blesses us?" "Oh? Well, it's just a form of expression, that's all darlin.'" "But does He bless us when we sneeze?" "Sure!" "Why don't we say 'God bless you' for other things, why just at a sneeze?" "Well, like I said, it's a form of expression and I'm sure we say 'God bless you' for other things. I've said it plenty of times at Bridge and to my family members. It's normal. Don't get hung up on it sweety."

The woman went back into her purse, took out a mask and covered her face. Ellen was beginning to get creeped out and opened the register. "Okay! All set sweety, here's your receipt." "Thank you!" "You're welcome!" "Can you put the pliers in a small brown paper bag?" "Yep, I already did darlin.'" "Oh, okay. Thank you!" "You're welcome. Here, lemme walk you out." Ellen escorted the woman out. When they made it outside, Ellen waved but the woman grabbed at her wrist.

"I don't mean to bother you, but can you tell me where I am?" "Where are you?" Ellen asked, startled. "Yes." "Well, for starters, you can let go of my wrist." Ellen tried to pull away but she didn't release the firm grip. She grabbed on tighter. "Uh..um...you're on White St. and that's Mt. Vernon Way. You lost?" "The woman let go of her wrist. "I think so." "Well, do you need me to call you a taxi? Or is your husband coming pick you up darlin?'"

"Oh no. Now I remember where I am! I need something else!" "Something else?" Ellen asked tentatively. "We're closed, as I've said before, but if you come back..." "If I come back tomorrow you'll be open bright and early. Yes, I heard you. But I need to go back inside for one more thing. It'll just be a few seconds. I thought that I just needed sharp-nose pliers. But I need a screwdriver too."

"Listen darlin' I don't mean to be rude but you need to leave! Especially since you look the way you do around here. It won't fair well." "Look...the way I do? What do you mean by that?" "I don't mean anything. Just be on your way." "Asian? Is that what you mean?" "Look darlin', no offense but the cops around here like to keep the streets clean. Again, no offense." "Clean?" "Yes! They don't like criminals out here of different colors doing God knows what, if you know what I mean. I was trying to be nice cuz' I'm not racist or anything, but the way you was grippin' my wrist, I don't know."

"You 'don't know?' Oh. I suppose you're right. What kind of city wants someone like me in it? Right? I should go back to my country perhaps." "I didn't say that but maybe...yeah...I dunno." "You 'dunno?' Wow. You sure are a woman of limited words.

I have an extensive vocabulary so if one were blind-folded, and we both had a conversation of any kind with them, they'd think that perhaps you were the one that needed to go back to your country. Perhaps a library? To pick up a dictionary? Study some words so you might not be shunned from a city."

"You calling me stupid, you bitch?" "I'm not calling you stupid, but you sure sound like it." "You better get your yellow ass off my street before I..." "Before you what? What are you going to do Ellen? Kill me? Bury me in your basement? Get some cement from out back and finish it off? Too late. It's already been done."

"Say whaaa..." The woman stabbed the pliers under the chin, plunging through the mid-line. She pushed it further and then ripped it out. Ellen fell to her knees but the woman covered Ellen's mouth. She stabbed Ellen with the pliers in the cheek and then in the throat.

She kept stabbing her until Ellen fell to the floor in a pool of blood. Walking into the store, the woman grabbed the gun underneath the register and shot Scooby straight in the head. Tyson ran out to see what was going on. "Who the fuck are you?" He yelled before she shot him in the leg and then the chest.

She placed the gun on the counter and left. When the police got there, they fingerprinted and took photos. Someone tipped off the police as to where Harvey was; charging him not only for the murders he was wanted for, but the murders of his stepmother, his nephew and his father. His fingerprints matched the ones on the gun and the pliers.

Harvey Duane Brandt was given life without parole. At the age of 74, a judge granted Harvey a mercy release due to the fact that he was old and dying of colon cancer. When he was released, no one came to pick him up so he walked.

A car honked the horn and a young girl stuck her head out. "Need a ride?" Harvey smiled and got in. He noticed that the woman was exceptionally beautiful. She turned on the radio. "I don't have anything to play so I hope the radio is okay?" "Yeah, sure kid."

"...Another head hangs lowly
Child is slowly taken
And the violence, caused such silence..."

Harvey kept looking down at the woman's crotch. He felt himself attracted to her and he just couldn't help himself. "Where were you just coming from?" She asked. "Looks like the prison?" "Yeah, I was doing some time for something but now I'm out, so it's whatever." Harvey grinned, putting his hand on the girl's leg. "Hey, you wanna take this grandpa to your place? I promise it all still works." He started to rub up and down her leg. "Gosh, you're pretty." When he looked down at her groin, he noticed that her white skirt was bleeding red.

"Hey! Looks like it's the time of day beautiful!" That's okay with me. I like that shit." "Oh? Is it?" "Yeah. Don't bother me none." "Lemme guess....you wanna smell it?" Harvey laughed. "You're reading my mind now?" "If I were reading your mind, I'd say you want me to sit on your face." "That's an idea." "Here's a better idea Harvey. Why don't we take a swim?" "A swim? Gee, I dunno, I just got out and I don't have anything to swim in. Wait...you know my name?"

"Sure. How can I forget your name?" The woman pressed her foot to the gas. "Whoa! You might wanna calm down there honey! You're going really fast." "Am I Harvey?" Harvey could smell her blood. The blood smell was pungent and it was filling the floor. "What the fuck is that?! What's going on? Hey, no sweat! Can you let me out at the next light?" "Aren't we going to swim Harvey?"

Harvey tried to open his door but it was locked. "Hey, can you do me a favor and unlock this door? Please?!" Harvey felt uneasy, panicking. "Well where are your manners Harvey? Didn't your mother teach you any manners? Or did she leave before you even started to talk? Poor kid. Left alone with his dad and some pedophile stepmother. Is that where you got your fetishes from Harvey?"

"Let me out of this fucking car you bitch!" The car was starting to fill up with blood. Harvey tried to hike his feet up on the chair but his legs were hurting and could barely move. "Careful Harvey you're an old man. Don't want you to break a hip. But maybe that won't be so bad! You like breaking bones, don't you?" "What are you talkin' about you crazy..." "So many bones. You are a serial killer, Harvey. Hmm?" "Where did you hear that?! Let me out of this fucking car! Where is this blood coming from?!" Harvey started to bang on the window frantically.

The blood was rapidly filling the car. "Please!! Please! I'm an old man! What do you want from me? I'm dying of cancer! Please! I just wanna go home!" The woman pulled over, reached across Harvey and pushed him out. He looked down at himself, and at the sight of being soaked in blood, he started to scream hysterically.

He got up and started to run down the road. And even though he was in a great deal of pain, he didn't want that woman to catch up to him. He saw a police station up ahead and ran into it. "Somebody help me!" He collapsed into the arms of an officer. When he awoke, he was in the hospital. He looked around and saw a nurse with her back towards him.

There was an officer beside him and his hand was shackled to the metal railing. He felt queasy and began to throw up on himself. "Take it easy!" The nurse said, grabbing Harvey and pushing his back and head forward. "I don't want you swallowing any of that, okay?" He caught a hold of her arm and said, "There was a crazy woman after me! She..she...was some crazy bitch...full of menstrual blood...so much blood...and it was fillin' up the car..." "Mr. Brandt? I need you to calm down." The nurse wiped up Harvey's vomit and injected a sedative.

When Harvey woke up, a woman hovered over him. She had her arms crossed, her hair wispy and completely white. She looked frag-ile but full of life with her nails done. She was sucking on a toffee candy and she spit it at him. "You're one unique son of a bitch Harvey. Did you know that the police called my house asking if you were a relative? A relative, can you believe that shit?

Do you really think that I would claim you as a relative after everything you've done? But I came anyway. As soon as I could too, Harvey. Cuz' turns out that even when you're given a second chance cuz' your asshole's got cancer, you still manage to catch a case. I wonder why they didn't let you rot in that jail cell. Why no one tried to slice your throat open in there, is beyond me!" "What case?" "Don't talk to me like you got the right to talk to me, you pig murderer!"

The officer put his hand up. "Calm down Mrs. Pruitt." "Oh, believe me I'm calm. As calm as an old broad like me can be when shit like this happens. Excuse my French officer but it's been a long day and a long time coming!" "Just take it easy. He's not going anywhere." "I just wanna give him the news."

Irene observed Harvey laying there and said, "You know all that blood on ya when you got to the police station? Somehow, it matched the DNA of some kid named Ruby you killed back in the 90's Harvey. Hey Harvey, how'd ya get fresh blood on ya from a murder in '93? That's some weird shit Harvey! You still into all that weird shit?"

"I didn't...I don't know what...you're talking about Irene." "The hell you don't Harvey. The hell you don't!" The officer warned Irene again about her tone. Irene snickered, placing another piece of toffee candy in her mouth. "You went up and killed my sissy, got my kid real good too. Then you got that good for nothin' Tyson. Gunned down in cold blood after all they'd done for you. Went and took my little boy you fucking monster. Was hoping you'd fry all those years but today is your judgment day, I do believe. For all your sins Harvey. You got a lot of them!"

145

"She was tryin' to kill me!" "Who? You losing your marbles? You killed all those people Harvey. That was you! They excavated that old house, you monster. They matched your DNA to some other stuff. You're gonna fry. Like a damn egg in a pan." Irene cackled, patting his shackled hand. "Won't bother to say 'God have mercy on your soul' cuz' He won't Harvey. What goes around comes around. All those evil things you did. Everybody knows now. You're gonna rot Harvey. Hell is hot and you'll be rotting there for all eternity for all the shit you did!"

Irene wiped her forehead and the officer escorted out. Harvey laid in that bed thinking about the woman in that car. He put two and two together and started to laugh maniacally. He looked over at the officer and said "I was sick back then. I'll admit it. I was a sick asshole. Had some big ol' demons runnin' through me...but don't we all officer? Ain't that right? Yeah, that's the past. And if they wanna fry me up and get me, so be it. But I got the cancer, so that'll get me first. You got a cigarette officer? Been dying for a smoke."

The officer shook his head in disgust. Harvey's eyelids grew heavy until he fell asleep. He was startled with a scuffle outside of his room. A male nurse ran into Harvey's room screaming. Harvey sprung up, nervously looking around. "What the fuck is going on out there?" He yelled to the nurse but the nurse hid behind a curtain. "Hey, did you hear me? What the hell is going on?" But he got no answer.

When Harvey looked out, he saw his officer lying in a pool of blood. He could hear yelling and then gunshots. "Justice!" Someone yelled. Another nurse flew over from gunshots trying to run into Harvey's room. The shooter walked into Harvey's room and got on his knees. "Harvey! Justice for Harvey! Hail Harvey!" Harvey was confused and scared. His whole body began to tremble.

"Hey kid...I dunno what you think you're doing...but..." "I'm doing this for you Master! Hail Harvey!" Suddenly, the police storm the hallway. The shooter pointed the gun at himself and pulled the trigger. Harvey started to scream. The blood and guts were sprayed on Harvey's arms and bed and he tugged violently on the shackles to no dismay. "Help! Someone help me!"

The police ran into the room and started to shoot. They shot 30 rounds. When the smoke subsided, Harvey was dead.

CHAPTER FIFTEEN:

FATHER FIGURE

My father's distance was perpetuated in guilt and defiance. Even those nights where he'd walk into my room and press my head against his chest with tears in his eyes, I knew there was an underlying fear. He didn't talk much, but when he did, it was about some movie we saw, about family or anything that would occupy his mind that he wanted to release.

He wasn't a man of many words. A sort of old-fashioned guy who relied on the bottle some days and then without drink for a while. He hated swimming and puffed on too many cigarettes. The arguments at home were endless where he'd give my mother a black eye and then he'd spend a few days at the local motel.

He'd return home, they'd make love and then explain that we'd never understand a lover's quarrel. That we were children and it wasn't up to us what happens in the household. We needed to mind our business and focus on school. I never quite understood why my mother never left him. She had a real problem grasping onto reality.

It was clear he was abusive and not right for her, but she says she stayed with him "for the kids." She didn't have to do us any favors. But we knew it was deeper than that. My father liked to keep us very private. We always lived in a house where the neighbors were never too close, and if they were, he'd have no problem uprooting us and leaving somewhere else.

I always thought it was because he wanted to spend time with us, but he was seldom home. And when he was, he spent his time in the basement. There was one night where my mother had to beg my father not to commit suicide. He'd made a noose around a pipe and threatened to end it all.

She was screaming and crying and after what seemed like an eternity, they'd come upstairs, go into the room and make love. There was this portentous dedication my mother had towards my father. Something incredibly morose and gruff. "Liam, I swear you have to stop, I swear it. We can't keep going on like this!" She'd yell from the kitchen.

She would throw a pot of boiling rice at him and he'd bang his fists on the table. We'd hide behind the sofa and stayed there until the coast was clear. Late at night, I'd hear the voices coming to me, often women telling me their stories and I'd just listen. At first, I thought I was hallucinating. My mom always told me I was a daydreamer. But those voices would corner me ill-timed until certain ones appeared, sitting on the foot of my bed, pleading with me to do something and help them. I could barely help my own mother and that always angered me.

My father was adamant about us attending church. We'd sit in the front row because we pretended we had nothing to hide. It was the only place he came alive. He would give riled up testimonies of stories we've never heard before; his lips pursed to the tip of the microphone. Feedback or not, he would sing a praise and worship song, his eyes closed, tears rolling down his eyes. He seemed to be really eager for forgiveness and salvation.

He made sure we were baptized; they'd bring out a large pool and one by one, lined up, they'd dunk us back after reciting some bible verse. I could see him looking from afar, proud of us, clenching his teeth, waving. It was so out of body to see him dedicate himself so deeply to this religion. It seemed credible and he looked like he was really trying and so, we went along with it.

When we'd get home, he'd make us dinner, we would laugh, play games and I'd bounce on his knee while he kissed my ears and say "I love you so much baby boy! My baby boy! You were made with so much love, you know?" He'd press his cheek to mine and it was the bond any father and son wanted AND needed.

Then something would happen where he would get upset at my mom and we would stop going to church all together. He would be on a pack a day again and my mother was falling down the steps, bruised up real bad. My sisters started to get it until the eldest ran off with some drug dealer. "I'm not sticking around for this shit!" She yelled into my father's face and slammed the door behind her.

My mother was starting to get tired of it as well. She started dating some guy named Oliver and she fell really hard for him. She would go dancing with him night after night while my dad spent his time in the basement fixing things and talking to himself. I started to get worried about his mental health.

One night I made myself some macaroni and cheese. And while the water boiled, I heard my father call out for my name: "Umezda come down here for a second, I need you to see this!" So I hurried down in my flip flops and poked my head out. I didn't see anything, so I went all the way down and said, "See what dad?"

"She's here. I can see her. She won't say anything. So we can't scare her away." "See who dad?" He stood there in his blue jeans and black t-shirt, hair long and tousled. Tears were coming down his face. "She's right here just being who she is." He said. I took a few steps forward but he put his arm out to stop me.

"Relax!" He said. Then he put down his arm and looked at me. "Bet you've always wondered why you got that name huh?" He asked. He put his arm around my neck and we walked upstairs together. "Dad you okay?" "Sure. I'm okay baby boy. You're so sweet. Such a sweet kid you turned out. I know...I know that I don't say that much cuz' your old man is a fuck up. But it's true. You're good. My only son you know?" "I know dad."

My father struggled with expressing his emotions quite often, especially when it came to me playing with dolls secretly. He'd walk into the room suddenly and catch me. He'd rip it out of my hands and would begin to scold me, then replace it with a G.I. Joe. I know he wasn't trying to suppress me or make me feel bad but that's what usually ended up happening. He tried to make sense of my personality and sense of humor and oftentimes he'd find himself judging me very harshly.

I wasn't hit very much, but when I was, it was followed by "Quit being a fucking faggot! I told you about that!" If I was washing dishes, he would press his knuckles into the back of my neck and say "Stop being a fucking faggot!" and drag me out of the kitchen. "Let the women clean that!" He'd say. I wasn't allowed to own anything pink or yellow. He even had my sisters brainwashed, making sure that if they saw something they should say something, and they always obliged. No worries though, because I always returned the favor.

Though I emptied most of my time reading books, trying to live out those fantasies, I knew once I looked away for a second, I was right back where I was, and that was a very oppressive and lonely place. I'd stare at my father from the hallway while he watched the news, his fingers slightly in his pocket, a cigarette hanging from his bottom lip. I just wished he was something more than that image.

"Your macaroni didn't come out too good Ummie. But I'll eat just because!" He laughed. "Dad?" "Yep?" He'd say, scraping the macaroni from the pan. "Why did you and mom name me 'Umezda?' Is it like some name you found from some science fiction book or something?" "No!" He quipped. "Why? Do kids say that shit at school?" "Kinda."

"Half those kids are gonna be morons when they grow up. They already are! Don't listen to them." "Then what does my name mean? Why couldn't I be Liam like you?" "Cuz' that's a stupid name. And Umezda is much cooler than Liam. Trust me." "So where did my name come from?"

"Well, I knew a girl...some friend I had years ago, before you kids were born. She was really into postcards. Like really nice, um... vintage postcards she collected. Well, anyway, she left one of those postcards in my car. She had a few names scribbled on that postcard and I asked her what those names meant.

She said that when she was pregnant, she liked the name Umezda. That it was unlike anything she'd ever heard. That it was a name for either a boy or a girl. She said she got that name from a dream." "A dream?" "Yeah. And that kind of always stuck with me. That name. I kind of liked it. And listen, your mom wasn't too keen on it. She gave me hell for it, but I talked her into it."

"You must've really liked this girl, huh?" "Oh yeah, she was pretty great. But again...it was way before I met your mother. It was another lifetime." "Another lifetime?" "Sure. So long ago. That's all gone. But I kept that part with me. So when I look at you...it all comes back...it reminds me. That's all. Now don't go running to your mom and telling her any of that, okay?" "I won't."

"And listen up. You're not really a faggot, so you know. I don't know where that comes from. I feel real bad when I say it. You're not that word. You hear me?" "Yeah..." "I mean it Ummie. You're not that word. I have this temper. I have this ugly side of me that comes out. It's like I see red. And it ain't right. I've tried to seek God for it cuz' it's bad. Your daddy ain't perfect. You hear me?" "I hear you daddy." "But don't hate me okay?" "I don't hate you dad."

CHAPTER SIXTEEN:

KNOWING

September 11, 2001

"Dr. Schigerr, I'm going to leave this cream of corn here. Now I know you don't like it, but you don't have to eat if you don't want to." "Can you bring me a bowl of Jello instead?" "I can certainly do that. Would you like me to put up the volume on your TV?" "No, no no. It's awful. It's just reruns...of...the towers falling and it's awful!"

"It's a really tough day in America. Maybe don't upset yourself?" Cathy changed the channel. "Looks like it's on all the channels huh? Here, I can turn it off." "No, no, leave it alone and get me my Jello." "Okay Dr. Schigerr, I'll be back in a bit." Cathy made her way to the kitchen and into the small refrigerator.

"Hey darling, would you mind bringing this up to Anatoly Schigerr in room 316?" "Yeah sure." Umezda made his way around the corridor and then up the steps. He tapped on the open door and then placed the Jello on the table. He smiled and said "There's your Jello. Bon Appetit!" "Can you take the wrapping off? I don't like the wrapping."

"Of course!" Umezda unwrapped the Jello and threw the wrapping in the trash. "There you go! Oh wait! I didn't get you a spoon! Be right back!" "No, no it's okay. I have a spoon over there. Can you grab it and put it in the Jello? I don't need you feeding it to me, I can do it myself."

Umezda laughed. "Yes sir. You look like you're capable of it! Anything else?" Dr. Schigerr pointed at the television and said "Pfff! This country is so lazy." Umezda shrugged. "So, you're good here?" "They should vote in, more Democrats. Reagan was trash. Bush was trash. Clinton was a good President, nevermind his indiscretions."

"I guess America likes to get it wrong a lot." "What's it say on your name tag there, young fella?" "Umezda." "Umezda? That's an odd name. Umezda. You know I used to be a Republican for a bit but I found out they tend to do things for the love of capitalism and not the love of the people. If it's not for The People then what a waste of time! Don't you agree?"

Umezda sat at the edge of Dr. Schigerr's bed. "I didn't vote. I mean, I should've but..." "You threw away your right to vote? Pfff! Youth these days. You'll soon regret it with that buffoon in office. Can't even spell. How's he going to handle this now? All those people...so sad!"

Umezda looked at the television and felt a sense of dread. "The real terror is human beings. We sure know how to fuck shit up, right?" "Language young man! Just because you're young, doesn't mean that is acceptable language." "You called our president a buffoon."

"Yeah, well, what kind of name is Umezda? You Russian? Sounds Russian to me." "My dad named me. He liked the name. There's not much to it. But I get that a lot. Maybe it is Russian." "Sounds familiar. Sounds very familiar." "Okay, so...I'm gonna head downstairs. Cathy is your nurse and there are a few aides on this level, so feel free to reach out to any one of them. Have a wonderful day uh..."

"Doctor. I'm a doctor." "Oh, cool. So, Doc…see you around." "Can't you stay a bit longer?" "I'd love to but I have some stuff to do downstairs and I'm a bit behind." "Not a lot of fellas that work here. They think the desired sex is the female for this kind of profession….but to be honest, I don't mind talkin' to a fella now and again. It's so chilly in here. These women know everything about me. I haven't seen a man in ages here. Did they die off?"

"I'm a fella." "Well, that's my point!" Dr. Schigerr made his way to his bed and dragged his spoon across the Jello. He put a chunk of it in his mouth and said "I had four boys." "Is that right?" "That's right!" Dr. Schigerr took another spoonful of Jello. "Francis, Anatoly Jr., Gregorio and Jonathan. All dead."

"Dead? I'm so sorry." "All dead. Yep! All dead. No daughters and I was happy not to have one. Girls are complicated. They get pregnant, leave home." "That's a bit archaic." "It's the truth kid. Women are complicated." "How did your sons die?" "That's quite a question. Sounds about personal. Maybe you should leave."

"I'm sorry. I thought that's where you were going with this story." "My twins Gregorio and Jonathan were the youngest. Both died in The Vietnam War. Francis died of a heart attack and Junior died during surgery for a facelift." "A facelift?" Umezda chuckled. "You gonna make a joke out of that?" "No, not at all. I'm sorry for your loss. Umezda covered his mouth.

"He was a sweet kid. Like to play with dolls, wear my wife's shoes etc. We knew what he was before he knew what he was. The sugar was there and we all knew it. But what do you do? It was The 50's and I was never home. Had to be the masculine figure representing the household. I used to blame myself."

157

"It's not anything to be ashamed of." "I wasn't ashamed of him. Not in the least bit. He took care of me before he died. Why do you think I'm here?" "He sounds amazing. You were lucky to have a son like that." "Maybe not lucky. Maybe blessed." "Maybe blessed. Yes!" "You have any kids? You look so young, maybe not."

"I don't think I can. I can't even get married." Dr. Schigerr tossed his bowl in the trash. "You can just give me the bowl so I can take it to the kitchen, or leave it there for Cathy to..." "I don't like Cathy. If she wants that bowl, she can fish it out of the trash like her men." Umezda laughed. "Why don't you like Cathy?" "Why can't you get married?"

"I'm Gay." "You like wigs?" "Uh, I don't wear them, no. Not sure how we got here." "If you ever want wigs, I have some in storage. Junior liked to perform." "Oh?" "Yeah, you know what drag queens are, right?" "Yes, I do." "Of course ya do! If you need wigs, I'm your man." Umezda scratched his arms nervously.

"Sounds good but just so you know, Gay men don't all wear wigs. Drag is an art form and being Gay is a sexual orientation. Two different things. I know you're like...older...but it's good to know. Never too late to educate yourself. I have to head downstairs." "Yeah, yeah, yeah. Thank you for the Jello, kiddo. Junior would've liked you."

"Thanks! Take good care Doctor." "Hey wait a minute..." "I really gotta split Doctor." "Wait...a...minute." Dr. Schigerr walked over to Umezda and got in his face. "Hey, what are you doing?" "Shhh! Just wait!" Dr. Schigerr analyzed Umezda's face and then slapped his shoulder. "You're him!" "Him?" Umezda stepped back.

"You're that guy! I know who you are!" "I told you my name.." "You told me we'd meet again. I thought it was a hallucination! But you're him! I can see it. You were a little older...you had a beard..." Cathy walked in with a glass of water. "Here, drink this and this." She moved Dr. Schigerr away from Umezda.

"You're being a bit aggressive Dr. Schigerr. Maybe you need to lay down?" "Get your paws off me nurse! I'm fine. More pills I see!" "Okay, I'm just trying to take precautions so you don't get your blood pressure up." "I'm perfectly fine." Cathy pressed her hand on Umezda's arm. "You okay? They can get testy sometimes. They're here all day so they get stir crazy.

You can go downstairs and read The Bible to the group. There's quite a few today." Dr. Schigerr stuck his middle finger out. "Oh, Doctor I thought we were starting to get along!" Cathy turned off the television and closed the door. She then went back in and took the bowl out of the trash. "Very funny."

"The ones on the second floor have all types of degenerative diseases and can at times do the most, so if that ever happens, just go to the main desk and buzz for a nurse." "Okay." Umezda scratched his head. "He said he's seen me before." "That's old age. It doesn't get pretty for them. The room is right along there. Thank you for reading to them. They love that. They need the stimulation."

Umezda sat down in a large white chair. He watched as the Senior Citizens signed in and sat on the chairs in front of him. He placed The Bible on his lap and smiled. Cathy came in with a microphone and had two men connect cables behind him. "I don't think that's necessary, I can project my voice."

"Some of them..." She pointed out to the crowd. "Are very hard of hearing so it definitely helps. We also don't want you to go hoarse. It's an hour read." "Oh, okay." Dr. Schigerr peaked his head into the room, sitting in the back row. Cathy rolled her eyes and walked towards him.

"I'll behave!" He yelled. "I just want to hear him speak." "That's what I like to hear. Would you like..." "I'm fine!" Bewildered, Cathy turned around, and before leaving the room, winked at Umezda and left. Umezda opened The Bible to Psalms 61. "This is my favorite passage because David is in despair. He feels out of place where he is and he seeks comfort from God. It is an assurance of God's eternal protection:

'Hear my cry O' God, attend to my prayer. From the end of the earth I will cry to You, when my heart is overwhelmed. Lead me to The Rock that is higher than I; For You have been a shelter to me. A strong tower from the enemy. I will abide in Your tabernacle forever. I will trust in the shelter of Your wings. For You, O' God, have heard my vows.

You have given me the heritage of those who fear Your name. You will prolong the king's life; His years as many generations. He shall abide before God forever. Oh, prepare mercy and truth, which may preserve him! So I will sing praise to Your name forever; That I may daily perform my vows.' Amen!"

Dr. Schigerr's eyes began to water. He wiped away the tears with his thumb and thought, "I need to speak to him privately." After the reading, Umezda made his way towards the exit. "Hey kid!" Dr. Schigerr yelled. "We need to talk."

CHAPTER SEVENTEEN:

UNREST

"26 year-old woman Tamika Sumley from Chicago was shot dead while she walked unarmed into a department store. The young woman was making a purchase when police mistook her for someone else. Tamika was gunned down while onlookers passed by. The footage was released early this morning by eyewitnesses who told police to stop shooting but they would not listen.

Tamika Sumley died at the scene. There are no details right now as to what The Chicago Police Department are going to do, but hundreds of protesters have gathered, chanting Tamika's name and asking for immediate justice. Tamika Sumley was the owner of Sum Of These Cupcakes Bakery and is coincidentally the daughter of Rosalind Sumley, a victim of serial killer Wilson Fabian Butler. She is also the sister of famous rapper Shawn SUMZ. The Sumley family currently has no comment but we will update you tonight with more details at 10."

Wearing a sweatshirt saying "Justice For Tamika," Shawn made his way across the hall and into his car garage. He took a deep breath and put on his mask. The mask said "Rosalind." As he pulled out, paparazzi snapped photos and shouted questions. "Will you seek justice for Tamika, Shawn SUMZ? How do you feel? You spend all day crying in your studio? Is it true your dating R&B singer Aniyah

Santiago? She was seen leaving your hotel last week!"

"Get out of the driveway yo!" He yelled, pulling out slowly. "Shawn, do you plan on inviting Beyonce and Jay-Z to the funeral? What about Drake? C'mon Shawn give us something." Shawn took a deep breath and said "Justice for Tamika" before finally making his way out. "Yo Raquel, do me a favor. Call my brother Austin and tell him to meet me later tonight. You know where." "Got it Mr. Sumley. Anything else?" "Yeah. Did you call the funeral and make the arrangements?"

"All set Mr. Sumley. I sent all of the details to your email. I also called your favorite florist." "I don't want all that bullshit over there, ya heard? I want it simple." "Simple. Yes, that's what we talked about. It's a very private service. I alerted the media that her funeral would be in Wisconsin to deter them, but I doubt they believed it."

"It's all good. Just make sure there's plenty of security there." "What about the protesters?" "What about them?" "Do you need security to clear them out?" "No, not at all. They can stay outside if they show up. They're showing my sister respect." "Yes they are sir." "Raquel...thanks ma. I appreciate all your hard work. I couldn't do this without you." "You are very welcome."

"And now a follow up on police shooting victim Tamika Sumley. An autopsy report concluded that she did not have any illegal substances in her body despite false allegations that she was under the influence and provoked Officers Benjamin Cork and Henry Lagialetta.

Although several pieces of evidence prove in footage that Ms. Sumley was not even facing the police at the time of the shooting, reports are being made in viral videos that Ms. Sumley was in a physical altercation and yelled obscenities to officers Cork and Lagialetta.

Here is part of the interview with Officer Lagialetta: 'We responded to the phone call that said the suspect had a red sweatshirt and jeans and was an African-American female. We responded with force because the suspect moved her arms and we felt threatened and fired.'

That threat was Ms. Sumley, removing the hangers from her clothing she was actively purchasing. Her receipt and interaction with the store cashier will also be part of the evidence against the two officers. This case is still under investigation. In other news, The President has caught the coronavirus."

As they lowered the casket, Shawn pushed his napkin to his nose; his eyes were bloodshot and his lips quivered. The pastor walked over to Shawn and hugged him for a publicity shot. "You're gonna be okay son." He said, as he faced the flickering cameras once more and then disappeared into his stretch limousine.

As the paparazzis clicked their cameras and reporters asked questions, Shawn kept his head down, lowered his mask and pressed his lips to the mic. "I appreciate all of the love and support that there is for my sister Tamika and my mother Rosalind Sumley." Shawn removed his jacket and handed it over to his assistant.

"While our family is actively grieving, I am overwhelmed with all the messages and we are all thankful to the protesters for demanding Justice for Tamika. These are some difficult times. We got a crazy ass president and some weird virus but we haven't lost our faith. We know that even in these trying times, we will prevail. Marcus Garvey once said:

'Emancipate yourselves from mental slavery, none but ourselves can free our minds.'

We know that this movement is not just for the advancement of black lives but for the fight against systemic oppression and racism of black and brown bodies and justice for and about them. We're tired of the police brutality and the cataclysm of erasure; we're plucked up from the root, suffocating in the instability and the mass manufacturing of white colonialism.

My sister is a black face; a real black face, not a comic strip or a minstrel show. She is the representation of struggle, and the identity of black men and women who exist, who existed and who WILL continue to exist when all is said and done. We demand justice for her murder but we don't march for the approval. We aren't interested in water cooler talk or the magic of stereotypical representation of repression; we want to walk down the street without being seen as a fucking threat.

I am my mother's son and my sister's brother. If that makes me a walking target then take out your guns and shoot me dead. Shoot me dead so that you have the satisfaction of holding onto your fake power. So that your kids can go to school without feeling like a big black rapper is out to get them. I'm so sick of trying to make sense of things. So sick of the hatred, but y'all white people are addicted to that racism.

Y'all would auction off slaves if it was made legal again. I'll leave y'all with this, a quote from James Weldon Johnson:

'It is a struggle; for though the black man fights passively, he nevertheless fights; and his passive resistance is more effective at present than active resistance could possibly be. He bears the fury of the storm as does the willow tree.'

I just want y'all to know:
I'M NOT JAMES WELDON JOHNSON. Rest in Power sis."

"This just in: Officers Cork and Lagialetta have been suspended without pay and will not be facing any charges. This coming off the heels of 13 year-old Lamar Ivory being shot in the shoulder for showing up to his friend's house in the suburbs. Police in Montana County say neighbors made disturbing phone calls that an African-American male was toting a gun and shooting at animals in the area.

Lamar Ivory's friend Emmett Zhane said that Lamar did not have any weapons except a book bag and a skateboard. Police are still investigating. Lamar is currently in the ICU at Langston Medical Center."

SNAKE IN THE RIVER

The ice cracked and swallowed him whole. His tiny hands flailing trying to make sense of the piercing cold water. Cobalt blue eyes cemented on her face as he swallowed huge gulps of water. His heart slowed down, choking the lungs, causing his tongue to swell. He descended beneath the sheet of ice, his nose pressed up in sudden unconsciousness. It was prompt and silent.

Only a roister of wind that circled the towering trees could bustle in the caliginous area. She looked, careful not to tip over. His little body drifted slowly in what seemed like an aphotic eternity. She sat at a distance and flicked open her book.

Reading to herself with a pocket flashlight, she smiled and said, "How genius!" Putting away the book in her long coat, she made her way towards the mouth of the cracked interstice. His little body had slid over uninterrupted, enough to see his face protruding through the icy water.

He stared into the sky in a locked gaze with the luminary moon and for a moment it scared her. She felt flustered and panicked. She went over near a tree and found an oversized branch, picked it up. Bungling with it, her book fell. She slowly slid the stick across the ice and the tip grazed across the water. His face brushed against the tip. "You're a bastard to make me feel this way." She lifted the stick and with all her might, struck the boy's face. She did it again and again until the water turned red.

Once she stopped, the boy's body disappeared beneath the sheet of ice again. She dragged the stick back to the wooded area and kicked dirt on it. She patted her coat and noticed that her book was missing.

A noise suddenly erupted. She turned her head and saw nothing but she knew it was something. She ran into the woods and slouched behind a large rock. Waiting to see if what the noise was, would appear, she put her coat over her head.

When the noise was gone, she slowly got up and made her way to the ice. She stood over the boy's body. She could see nothing more than a swell of red. Her heart raced. "What if they find him and he says something?" She thought.

She threw herself on the floor and plunged her arms into the freezing water. She reached deep to feel his shoulder. She pushed him down but he kept afloat. "Fuck!!!" She yelled. Suddenly she heard a dog barking and she fled. Running, she slipped and hit her head.

She looked down at her hands when she felt the pain. She ran her fingers through her hair. "Oh my God. I left my blood here! They're going to find me and put me away." She got up and ran off. She ran and ran until she saw the street she came through.

Getting into her car, she turned it on and pulled away. "What if someone saw my car?" She brooded as she drove, feeling damp disgust. She wanted to rid her body of him. She could feel his eyes digging into her. "I was never raised like that." She whispered. When she got into her driveway she noticed that her neighbor was sitting on his front porch.

"Fucking loser. Die already." Her neighbor had a beer in his hand and waved. "You coming from work Kylie?" "I'm always coming from work." She quipped. She ran up the steps and into the bathroom, immediately taking her clothes off. She looked in the mirror and felt for the lump behind her head. She then turned on the shower and stood there for 15 minutes. She climbed into her bed in a desultory fashion, no remorse and fully exhausted.

When she woke up, she looked over at the time. "Fuck, it's noon. I overslept! Ugh!" Her answering machine had five missed calls and three messages. "Kylie, where are you? Something terrible has happened. Please call me back!" Beep. "Kylie where are you? Call me back! Quick!" Beep. "Oh my God Kylie you need to pick up the fucking phone already! It's Elia.

Please call me, this is like not even funny! It's an emergency!" Beep. The phone rang four times and then she heard her sister's voice. "Kylie? Did you just wake up? I called you like twenty times!! I need to know if you've seen Brandon."

"Why would I see Brandon?" She asked. "I dunno! I'm just really scared but I'm trying to think positive you know? I mean, I woke up and everyone was at breakfast except for him. He was in bed last night, and he's six so where the fuck would he go? I'm confused. I want to call the cops but I want to make sure he's not in the house.

I even checked the basement and he's not here. I'm hoping he went for a walk because I know he loves the snow but it's freezing and it's a Sunday so.." "Well I think you're overreacting. He's probably somewhere playing with his toys. Did you check the attic?" "Yes I checked the attic! I called his friends and no one seems to know!

Kylie I'm really scared and I don't know what to do!"

"Calm down Elia you sound intense. Maybe you need to calm down and then call me back. Take a Xanax..." "What? Kylie you're my sister and I need you right now!! I can't find him and I'm freaking out! I'm just hoping he's somewhere near. I think I'm going to call the cops now."

"No! Don't call the cops! They make a big deal out of everything, especially during the weekend. And what if he's at a friend's house and the cops think you're just some crazy soccer mom who likes to bullshit. The cops would never come to your house again." "I'm just really scared. Ralphie and Diana are scared too. I'm trying to put them at ease but I need to find him. Can you come over?"

"Um...okay yeah sure. Let me take a quick shower and I'll drive over. Gimme like an hour." "An hour? Kylie I need you NOW!" "Okay lemme throw some jeans on." Kylie hung up the phone. She couldn't breathe. She felt flustered and annoyed. She thought about ending her life by hanging herself or putting a bullet in her head. This would be much easier than getting found out.

She looked over at her pillow and saw a large dry spot of blood. She quickly tossed it in the laundry bin and drove over to her sister's house. When she got there, a cop was talking to Elia. "Oh my God. Oh no. I have to drive away from here right now." She thought. She started to judder and held on tight to the wheel to keep her nerves calm.

She closed her eyes and all she could see was his blue face sticking up looking out from under her. She eagerly wanted to laugh but she covered her mouth. She started to shake and she ran her fingers across her chest. She felt perversely aroused by the excitement. "I'll get caught but It'll be worth it." She thought.

She took a few deep breaths and finally got out of the car. She brushed past the cop car and waved to her sister. Elia was fidgeting with her stone-washed jacket talking to the cop. "Isn't it a bit cold to talk to him out here sis?"

"Kylie!" Elia embraced her sister. "Officer Hoyt, this is my sister Kylie. I called her as soon as I knew he was missing." The officer nodded and put his hand out. Kylie shook it and they all walked inside. "So you said that Brandon was sleeping last night. That was the last time you saw him?" Elia nodded. "Elia, tell him the truth."

Elia turned and looked at Kylie bewildered. "The truth?" "Yes, the truth. You had a crazy ex-boyfriend who used to threaten you all the time, remember? Tell Officer Hoyt the truth so he can help you." Elia, stunned, responded "I haven't seen or heard from Harvey in over four years. Why would you even bring him up?" The officer shook his head and said, "Ma'am we need those kinds of details in order to figure out what happened to your son.

We want to make sure we connect those dots so that finding him is much easier. Now did Harvey ever threaten the lives of any of your children?" Elia gasped. "Um, no I don't think so. Maybe." "Elia, you know that Harvey was verbally...and physically abusive. You told me that he said he'd burn your house to the ground with you and the kids in it. That sounds like a credible threat."

Elia put her hand on Kylie's leg. "What are you doing? Why are you doing this now? I haven't heard from or seen Harvey in forever! I don't remember ever telling you that he said that." "But you did tell me that Elia. You have to make sure officer Hoyt knows every- thing so that he can do his job. I'm sure he's going to contact Harvey and make sure he has nothing to do with it. But we can't ever be too sure."

"She's right Ma'am. Look, before we get into Harvey, what was Brandon wearing?" Elia's hands began to tremble. She felt something was horribly awry and started to sob. "Uh...um, I'm sorry what?" "What was Brandon wearing?" "Okay...he was wearing his dad's old black t-shirt, his Spiderman underwear and uh...I showed you his picture, he's thin, brown hair, dark blue eyes. He has a birthmark on his inner left thigh. The shape of a star almost. Um...I don't know what else you need, just please find my baby!"

Kylie withdrew a cigarette. "Can I smoke in here, sis?" "Smoke? You're smoking now?" "I started recently." "Kylie, do you think you know where your nephew is?" "He's at the bottom of the lake hopefully." Kylie thought. She wanted to scream it out and then laugh in their faces and say, "You're gonna find my blood on that fucking ice because of that damn dog and my book too! A good book that I never finished! Ha! But you cops are so damn stupid you'll never put two and two together."

"I don't know Officer. I haven't been to this house since last Thursday. He's very social and he has a lot of friends so he could be at one of their houses. He's always playing video games and these days kids get involved with complete strangers playing along. Elia is very good with supervision but you can't ever be too careful, right? I told my sister not to overreact. I don't want her to stress. She's been through a lot as a single mother." "Well, it's quite common that mothers overreact when their kids go missing. I'm assuming you don't have children, correct?" "No I don't, but I have two nephews and a niece and they can be a handful. I wouldn't make a great mother officer. I've always had to work hard. We don't come from privilege. But I resent that!" Kylie smiled.

The officer smiled and winked at Kylie. "Well, I'm sure you'd be an excellent mother." After taking down info, the officer left and

Elia slammed the door. "What the fuck was that? Do you even know what you said to that guy? Do you know that me and Harvey are making up and you just ruined that for us. You know he's on parole again and that's going to fuck up whatever we have. He CANNOT be a suspect!"

Kylie knew how to play on her sister's desperation for men. Accusing Harvey was a better idea rather than confessing that she killed Brandon. "Listen to yourself Elia. You're defending a man when your son could be dead out there." "Dead? What? Why would you even say that? He's not dead!" Elia kicked the side of her sofa.

Bringing up Harvey and all? You can't be a fucking idiot right now, you just can't okay? And then you smoke in my house? Since when? This is a time when I really need my sister to show up and act like she fucking cares and not like some asshole giving a show for the cops. My kid is somewhere and you're acting like this. Were you flirting with that cop?!"

"Flirting? What? Gross. I'm here right? You called me and I'm here. Listen, I'm not good at these things. I'm super awkward and that cop made me nervous. I'm gonna be right there every step of the way supporting you. We're gonna find him sis, I promise. And you know I hate cops, so don't ever in your life."

"Okay. Okay! I'm just in my head. I want to know where my baby is. Do you think he went over to your house and you missed him on your way here?" "I doubt that. He's six and he doesn't walk long distances. I'm half way across town. Are you sure it wasn't Harvey or one of your boyfriends? Where is Harvey?" "One of my boyfriends? He's...I dunno. We had a small fight and we made up and he probably went to that sleazy bar. I don't care. Brandon was not with him."

"Well you better find out sis. You can't let a man dictate your life.

You're so fucking weak these days." "I know, I'm just trying to manage the pizza shop and make it home in time for the kids when they come home from school. I've been tired and my mind is all over the place. But I put Brandon to bed last night. I promise!"

"I know sis." Kylie pulled her sister close lugubriously and said, "Are the kids upstairs?" "Yeah?" "Go get a shower, I'm gonna do the same and we can look for Brandon together in a bit, okay? I really need a shower." "Do it here." "I didn't bring any of my clothes and last night I had someone over so I need to clean up and..." "Okay, do your thing. I'll call mom and give her the news. I'm so scared Kylie, like, this is all...this is all too much!"

"Relax. We're gonna find him. Okay? I'll be back as soon as I shower...okay?" "I love you Kylie." "Awe E, you know I love you more. Don't stress. He'll show up." Kylie got in her car, slammed the door and put both hands on the wheel. The adrenaline running through her veins was something she'd never felt before.

She backed out of the driveway, wiping her sweaty palms on her thigh. She cracked the window to smoke a cigarette furtively and took a deep pull. Kylie drove watchfully until she got out of the city. She kept driving until she saw a sign for Chicago. She pulled into a McDonald's and parked. When she went inside, she ordered a quarter pounder and a parfait. She sat at a table right across from a college student who was writing in her notebook. "Hey, I'm sorry but I was wondering if I could ask you a question?"

The girl looked up and smiled. "Sure!" "I'm Vivian and I just moved to Chicago and I was just wondering if there were any good bars here. I missed brunch but I'm having this burger so..." "Hmm, I think there's a bar called Heatherly's four blocks from here. There's also a bar called Dice's but it's kind of sketchy." The girl laughed. Kylie pointed at the notebook. "Do you go to college around here?"

"Yeah." "Oh cool! I'm a Journalist. I see you're writing a paper. Wow, it's been forever since I wrote a paper." "Well I'm just doing some homework." "Oh okay. Well thank you for pointing me in the right direction. I'll let you know how it goes if I ever see you again. What's your name again?" "I don't think I told you. It's Emiko, nice to meet you Vivian."

"Do you mind me asking what your ethnicity is?" "Not at all. I'm Japanese-American. My mother is Japanese and my father is Irish-American." "That's probably why you're so beautiful." "I appreciate that but I have a boyfriend." Kylie drove to a remote spot and fingered Emiko. The windows fogged and her arm was tired but when she heard Emiko cum, she felt redeemed. "Thank you for that Vivian. I didn't know I needed that." "The pleasure was all mine."

Kylie drove to a phone booth nearby. She put the coins in the slot and pressed each number. She waited until she heard a distinct voice. "Harvey?" "This ain't Harvey. Who is it?" She hung up and tried another number. "Hello, can I speak to Harvey?" "Harvey ain't here. He's at his place. Wanna leave a message?" "No thanks." She didn't think he'd be home but turns out he was. "I called your parent's store. Your mom's a real peach." "What do you want?" "What do you mean, what do I want?" "I'm not up for a fuck, I just had a girl over. She's still here." "You better lose her Harv, I've got some business to finish with you."

"Business?" "Yeah weasel. Business. What? You got wax in your ears?" "Okay so?" "He's dead Harvey. And I want the money. And I want it wrapped in newspaper like I told you before. Don't make me overextend myself. You know I hate doing that." "Gimme a sec... Bailey go down and get us a few beers down at the liquor store, I'm talkin' here."

"Okay, so are you fucking out of your mind? I'm already with your sister. Like, the whole fucking point was to get her to go back with me. And I did that." "I knew you were going to be a pussy." "Hey relax okay? Elia is a good woman and I just wanted to scare her a bit." "You asked me to kill my nephew...for you. And I did. So?"

"You really are a fucking psychopath, aren't you?" "Takes one to know one Harvey. Want me to give names? I'm not a tattle tale buddy. So get those dollars wrapped and don't think I don't know the difference between fake and real. Don't try to fool me. And don't get your bitch mother involved. If the cash is coming from her, tell her it's some important business. Are we clear?"

"Are you sure the kid is dead?" "He's underneath some lake right now. You have the location. Leave the money there...'you have one minute remaining'... Harvey? You there?" "I'm here." "The money. Today." "How did it feel?" "To be honest...fucking fantastic!" "I told you. I just didn't think you'd actually go through with it."

Kylie walked to Dice's and had herself a few drinks. She drove back home and waited. Her phone had six messages but none of them were from Harvey and that was a good thing. Kylie then grabbed her duffel bag and tossed it in the backseat. She drove to the location she gave Harvey.

She put on some lipstick and swept her hair into a ponytail. She didn't feel nervous at all. She remembered one of her sister's messages: "I can't believe you would ditch me when your nephew is missing. This is the fucking worst Kylie. I needed you more than ever and you abandoned me. Call me back when you get this message." You selfish bitch."

Beep. Kylie waited patiently, slipping in a cassette of "Nothing Compares 2 U" by Sinead O'Connor. After a while, she stepped out and grabbed the bag. She got inside her car and opened the bag.

The money was all there. Kylie laughed and turned up the song. She placed the bag on the passenger's side and began to pull away.

Suddenly, there was a loud tap on the side of her car and she stopped. It was a tall man waving frantically. She rolled down her window slightly. "What?" She yelled. "Harvey said Hello." The man pulled out a gun and shot Kylie four times. She slumped over and accelerated the gas. She crashed into the side of an abandoned building.

The man walked up to her and pressed the gun to her forehead and pulled the trigger. He went around the passenger's side, opened the door and took the money. The man got into his car and drove until he saw an ill-lit payphone. "Is it done?" "Yeah it is." "Okay, head on over Wilson, and I'll give you your cut. You did good. Did she struggle?" "Nope. She went down pretty easy." "Good. That's great news. She thought she was going to run me. Okay head on over." "You got it boss."

The next day, Harvey made his way to Elia's house and he assured her they'd find her son. A week later, Brandon's body was found in the icy lake. Elia assumed that Kylie was also a victim of the same murderer. Harvey promised to marry her and eventually he did. They were married for less than a year before she found out that there were some murmurings that Harvey was acting inappropriately with young children. People were also insinuating he was involved in some money laundering schemes.

Rather than confront Harvey, she quietly divorced him and decided to move to another city. She found a good job and she was able to raise her kids there. For years, Elia struggled with her mental health. She never confronted her pain. And now that her children were teenagers, she decided to attend a meeting for women who were trying to cope with the loss of a loved one.

"Elia, if you feel comfortable, please feel free to share your story. But only if you're ready to face it. If you want to do it another day, that's perfectly fine." "No, today is fine...thank you. It's really so hard to say out loud because...I've never really told anyone...how I feel. I guess this is the place to do it, but if it gets too hard, then I'll just stop. Is that okay?"

"Of course!" "Okay. Well, my name is Elia." "Hi Elia!" The crowd shouted. She smiled nervously. "Hi. My instinct is to put my hands in my pockets cuz' I'm nervous but I'm not going to. So here it goes: My son Brandon was murdered. My sister Kylie was also murdered soon after by the same killer. To this day they've never caught him.

It's absolutely frightening to say that because I worry for my kids every day. I'm just...so scared sometimes that I have to check the locks like fifty times to make sure we're safe. If the wind is rattling the windows, I sometimes think he's trying to get in. But nobody is there.

There are times when I have mixed feelings about everything because some things don't add up, but I just tell myself that justice will be served...one day. Brandon was..." She gulped. "My baby was six when they took him out of his bed. They...um...he was at the lake and uh..."

"It's okay Elia. You don't have to give those details. Just tell us how you feel. We're here to help you cope." "Okay..thanks...um....I do miss my baby like...every day. There's not a day I don't go into my purse and pull out his blanket, from when he was a baby and smell it. I refuse to ever give that up because it's the only way he's truly with me. I mean, who loses a child like that? You know?"

Elia wiped her tears. "Here's a tissue. You're doing great." The Counselor said. "I can't trust people. I have a real problem confiding in and understanding that not everyone is out to get me and my two kids. I'm overprotective. I'm needy when I date men and then I lose them quickly because it affects me day to day. Not to say it's always me, cuz' some of these men are a trip! Some days are better than others. I don't drink because I need to be clear for my children.

But sometimes I see the bottle of wine and I wanna purchase it. I know it'll mimic easing the pain but I need more than that. I need... healing. It's a cruel world and I'm just trying to get by with my kids and I wanna live for myself too not just for them. But it's hard. It's hard when they need book bags and clothing and trapper keepers and lunch money.

I had to get on Welfare for a bit when I went part time but luckily they promoted me to full time so I'm happy about that. I'm just...I just miss my son. I miss my best friend, my sister. I miss her face, calling her. I don't think I can ever get that image out of my mind, how she died. It's all so sad. But...anyway, that's all I have for now. Thank you for listening."

"Thank you for sharing your story Elia. We appreciate that very much. You'll find here that we aren't providing solutions to these losses. A loss is forever and it leaves an indelible mark. We confide in one another because these people we lose, they stay alive because of us. This is proof of existence when we know time wants others to forget. But we don't. These are our mothers, sisters, daughters, fathers, brothers, aunts, uncles, friends etc.

Here, we deal with all of it. So that maybe we can sleep better at night knowing, you're not alone. Let's give a round of applause for Elia. Next up we have Josie. Josie is also new here so give her the same love we gave Elia." After a small applause, Josie stood up. She looked at Elia and smiled. "I can't imagine losing two people like that. Thank you truly Elia for being so brave and speaking up like that.

I wanna say that I lost my sister very young. I don't know how to put it into words because it happened so quickly. She was with her boyfriend and then she disappeared forever. The police didn't really make much of an effort to find her and I spent a lot of my time resenting my mother because of it. Because she didn't do more for Jacinda.

It's so frustrating because I miss my sister every day. I want to be able to call her and say 'Hey you have some beautiful nieces who look just like you.' I wanna be able to hold her hand again and laugh and watch those movies we watched. She loved movies. She could've been a movie star, she was so beautiful.

I idolized her. I wanted to style my hair like her, I loved her dresses. They were always so pretty. She knew how to wear a dress. She had this spark that was so unique. Such a beauty. I don't remember a day she ever made me feel less than. Just an awesome big sister.

I resent my mother for not going after her boyfriend who was the prime suspect. That really grinds my gears. My mother spent a lot of time trying to cope and figure shit out. Oops! I'm sorry! Can I say shit?" "Go on." "Anyway, the guy left town. We never saw him again. The whole town knew but the cops never did a damn thing.

It became too much. Everywhere I went, people asked me about her. She was an urban legend. It was literally making me sick. I decided to leave town after my mom did, found this place and fell in love with it. It's a far cry from the bland and boring cookie-cutter suburbs. And like Elia, I'm raising kids and I want what's best for them. I didn't need to be some place where people immortalized the disappearance of my sister.

I miss her every day and I'm hoping that I can deal with it better. Because it still eats away at me. And unlike Elia, I have turned a few times to the bottle...I have. Almost lost my marriage because of it. I just hope one day, that they find where she is so we can give her a proper burial. That's all." Jacinda sat down and settled her hand on her cheek. Elia felt sorry for her.

After the meeting, Elia approached Josie. "Hi I'm Elia!" "Hello, I'm Josie, nice to meet you!" "Likewise. Your story was really something. We both lost sisters. I didn't think I'd meet someone who felt the same way as I did, as strange as that sounds." "Oh no, likewise. You losing two in one is really sad. You said a lake? I don't know how you're still standing." "Faith, I guess."

"How long have you lived here?" "I'm going on five years." "Really? I've been here about eleven or twelve years. It's a great place." "I haven't made a bunch of friends but we should definitely hang out. I was very social back then. I need to get back to that. Been doing the mom thing too long, not that I don't love it. But I need some fun."

The two laughed and grabbed bagels. "Oh they have everything bagels! Yum!" Elia laughed. "I love everything bagels too! I will sometimes substitute raisins but everything is pretty on the money." "So your sister has been missing since like...when?" "1976. Yours?" "Mines didn't go missing. She was murdered in 1990."

"Oh wow, that's not too long ago. I'm so sorry. Well, I'm glad you're here with me. Here's my number. Feel free to give me a ring anytime before 7pm. Kids come home and after 7pm I'm exhausted. Unless Dennis wants to be a babysitter. That's the husband." "Does he have a brother?" "Yes, but he's bald and short." "He sounds like my type." "Oh good!"

CHAPTER NINETEEN:

NO SLEEP FOR THE WICKED

Umezda tossed and turned that night. He couldn't get the imprint of Blaire out of his mind. He threw some pillows around and tucked them under his feet, pushing some blankets around and trying to fall asleep but it all became too difficult. He fumbled about, grabbing the remote control. He tried to watch some television but there were only reruns and bronzer infomercials.

"Ugh!" He ran down the stairs, rummaged through his pantry and found some candles. He looked at the clock: 3:16am. Then he began to light them. He placed them throughout and sat on the floor with his eyes closed, meditating. He didn't know exactly what he was looking for but he was trusting his gut instincts. He took shallow breaths into his chest and exhaled slowly. He tried to calm his trepid imbalance.

He stretched out, placing both palms flat on the cold floor. He waited. And he was on standby. Nothing. He adjusted his lotus position and took another shallow breath inwards. He respired slowly. "Blaire, if you can hear me, I want you to show yourself. I know you're scared but you have all the time you want to express yourself. Feel free to do so."

He zealously awaited, but the floor was still cold and it made his bones sore. He got up and walked around the room freely, then towards the window where Blaire made her presence known. He backed away and then went into the same previous position. "You can say something if you'd like Blaire, anything. I can help you. I can guide you. I can listen."

He closed his eyes and moved forward, his forehead thrusted against the wood. Suddenly, the floor got tepid. The wood flushed in a soft glow. He didn't open his eyes for fear of breaking the connection. He could feel someone or something was there. "Blaire is that you?" He yelled out.

There was no answer. "Maybe this floor is warm because I keep touching it. I'm psyching myself out. She's not coming back. She probably needs a vessel and because I'm a man, she's not going to use me. Also, I probably won't remember, so..." He smelled something sweltering and when he opened his eyes, there was a hand holding one of the candles.

He was startled for a second but kept his composure. "Blaire is... is that you? You are safe here. No one is going to harm you." He hesitated closing his eyes for fear of losing the spirit, but he did it anyway. He could smell the candle getting closer to his face and he was afraid, whatever it was, would melt it right off. "I WANT TO SPEAK TO HIM." The voice said thunderously, causing Umezda to slide across the room.

He skid backwards, tears of true fright were rolling down his eyes. "What are you? Who are you?" He asked fearfully. "EDDIE." "Eddie?" He repeated back shakily. "Whaaat...what....who is that?" The spirit came closer with the candle. Suspended midair, it rattled the floor and cracked the ceiling like a walnut shell . "I NEED TO SPEAK

TO HIM." "I don't know who that is!" "YOU KNOW!" "I know?" The candle exploded and Umezda ran out of the room.

"I don't know what you want! I don't know what you are!" He said as he made his way up the steps, into the bed and under the covers. He began to hyperventilate until he calmed himself down. Once he was calm, he managed to fall asleep. Then something started to tug on his blanket. First slowly and then completely, ripping it away from him and into the air. He started to scream, falling out of his bed and crawling towards the bedroom door.

The blanket was spinning in the air until it fell flat on the bed. "BRING ME TO HIM." The voice said, screeching in his ears, his body in a fetal position from the terror. Umezda thought he was going to pass out from the fright. Then suddenly, his fingertips felt clammy as if he'd been digging out of the ground with his bare hands. His eyes widened, his back contorting, flinging him into the air. He began to spin, crashing onto the ceiling and then the sides of the walls, knocking things over with his head, hands and legs. His mouth felt like it was on fire; as if he had eaten ash or soil. He could feel the grit in between his teeth, his ribs contracting and his heart pounding out of his chest.

He fell back onto the bed and closed his eyes. After a moment of silence, he opened them up again but he was not himself. Jacinda blinked profusely, she touched Umezda's skin as her own. A reminder of the youth she once had. She stretched the arms out, then the legs. Without hesitation, she walked towards the bedroom door and then down the steps.

She could feel his supernatural energy tussling about in his head, shaking her to come out but she couldn't just yet. "I need your help Umezda. I'm not trying to hurt you. I need you to take me to him." She said in a vibrated echo. Umezda's throat felt itchy, his pulse was racing. "Why me?" Umezda asked. "He can't see me. He doesn't have what you have. I need to finish what he started."

"But who is Eddie?" "Don't you know?" "I told you that I don't." "He's your father." "No! No, my father is Liam Wicker. You're not listening!" "That's not his real name." "What? Listen, I can't have you inside of me. This has never happened to me before. I can help you, but you can't use me like this. I didn't give you permission..." "I don't need your permission." "What are you going to do?"

"You'll find out soon enough." Jacinda looked in the mirror and saw Umezda: tall, good looking, sympathetic eyes. She went into the kitchen clumsily and saw a butcher's block. She pulled out a knife and said, "Take me to your father." "No! No, you have a knife. You want to kill him! He didn't do anything wrong! You've got the wrong person!"

Jacinda pressed Umezda's fingers across the side of his face. Then she pressed his fingers against his lips. "Do you feel that?" "Feel... what?" "The pain." "I...I don't know what..." Then suddenly, Umezda felt a sharp blow across his face. He held out his hands because there was so much blood.

He fell to his knees crying. "What is this?" "Your father's work, Umezda. Your father killed me." Umezda jolted, he started to shake and he could feel his neck crack. "Everything that you feel, I felt. He took my life. He took my life and I was only seventeen." Umezda's arms flung out and a surge of energy rippled out of his fingertips.

The electricity bounced across the walls and shattered the windows. "He took me to the same abandoned park he took you and your sisters...year after year Umezda! Your father is a MURDERER!" Umezda felt the words spew out of his lips. He felt his body rising and then crashing onto the floor. "I'll take you to him! Please!

I don't want to feel this anymore! Please!"

Jacinda calmed her sensory and the pain was gone. "I want to speak to him. Just the three of us. He needs to know." Umezda pointed to the car keys and they got into his Toyota. "Are you going to kill him?" Jacinda sat inside him tacitly. Umezda's eyes were out of focus and he couldn't pay attention to the road.

"Look, he's always kinda been...sad. And I don't know if..." "Don't make excuses for him. Everyone is sad. Look around you. It doesn't matter what time it is or what year has come and gone Umezda. We're all sad. He needs to right his wrong. HE WILL RIGHT HIS WRONG!"

"Yeah...yeah, okay you're absolutely right!" Umezda wanted to veer off, but Jacinda's hands were uniform on the steering wheel. "You have to understand Umezda that I was stolen away from what was mine. My family, my friends, my future. He took it. He felt he was allowed to have one but not me."

As Umezda drove, he finally realized that this spirit was Josie's sister. It hadn't occurred to him because he was so scared. "I can drive you to your sister. I know where she lives! Maybe you can re-unite with her?" Umezda suddenly felt a heaviness in his heart. He started to sob and then he could feel her crying out for Josie.

"I feel your pain...literally...I feel it Jacinda. I can't explain that kind of affliction. It's like being..." "Like losing everything you have." "Yes..." Umezda saw his father's car parked out front and pulled in behind it. "Please! Please Jacinda, whatever you're going to do, please don't let me see it. Please! He's...my father."

Umezda pressed the key to the lock and turned it. He could feel Jacinda eager to twist the knob. The house was dark. The only sound that was there was his footsteps and the clock ticking away in the dining room. The clock clicked louder than usual, but then again, this was all phenomenal and grim.

Umezda made his way up the stairs and then faintly down the hall. "He's in there." Umezda whispered. When Umezda looked down, he realized he wasn't walking but gliding along on his toes. He was disturbed but kept going.

He felt his fists clench and his hand tightening around the knife. He knew that she was there to kill him. But he couldn't do anything about it. Umezda was stark white, he could taste his and her tears. "It'll look like I killed my own father..." He cried. "Wake him up." Eddie was lying there, shrouded in patterned sheets, snoring away.

"Dad?" Umezda hid the knife closely behind his back. "Daddy?" Eddie turned over and swatted into the air. Then there was the snoring again. "Dad, I really need you to wake up..." Eddie kicked out one foot and opened his eyes startled. "Holy shit! Ummie? You scared me half to death! Are you okay? What's wrong?!" He reached over to turn on the light but Umezda stopped him, grabbing his wrist.

"Will you let go of me so I can turn on the light? What's wrong?" "I'm sorry Daddy I can't do that." Umezda steadily pulled his arm from behind him and revealed the knife. Eddie backed away from him, petrified. "Whaaaa...wait Umezda, what are you doing?! Oh my God Ummie, what are you..." "Daddy please! I need you to listen to me!" Umezda's hands were shaking profusely. He could feel the sweat dripping down the tip of the knife.

There was absolute terror in that room shared by both father AND son. "Oh God...Oh God..." Eddie repeated. "You're gonna kill me? Oh, baby please! What did I do?" "Daddy you have to stay calm please. Please!" "Oh no, baby please don't do what you're planning to do...oh my God..." "Daddy please...CALM DOWN!"

"Calm down?! You have a large knife! Is that a knife? I can't see in this dark!" "It's...a knife. But you have to be quiet and listen, okay?" "Yeah kid, I'm listening..." "She's...come for...YOU." "What? Who? Did you lose your mind Umezda? What are you talking about?" Jacinda swung the knife into the air to get his attention. Eddie curled into a ball. "Oh my God Ummie...baby please!" Eddie began to sob, reaching for his phone but he realized it was next to the lamp on the other side. "Hello Eddie. Remember Me?" "Huh?" "I saved you the trip." "What are you talking about Ummie?"

"Don't act surprised. We both knew this time would come." "What?!" "Dad! It's Jacinda." "What?! I'm confused! I don't know any Jacinda! Put that knife down!" "SHUT UP!" She yelled. Umezda's eyes lit up like fire. Eddie started to scream, clinging to the bed frame. "What the fuck..."

Umezda began to levitate, he moved around the bed and towards his father. His body was there but it was no longer him. Jacinda had taken over completely, pressing her lips against Eddie's ears. "Liam Wicker? Or is it Eddie Sokoloff?" Eddie began to tremble. Jacinda pressed the knife to his shoulder. "I asked you a question. Is it Liam Wicker or Eddie Sokoloff?"

"It's...Eddie." "I figured." Jacinda moved the knife upwards towards Eddie's throat. "Liam. Eddie. Maybe those are not your names." "Whaa..what do you mean?" Eddie kept his eye on the tip of that large knife. "Maybe you're just a CREEP. Remember that? CREEP?" Jacinda pressed the tip of the blade gently against his jugular. Eddie let out a whimper.

"CREEP. That sounds so much better. I mean...that's the word that got us into this mess, right? CREEP?" Jacinda stepped back and put her arm down. "Maybe you're just weak. Ever think of that?" Eddie peed on himself, the hot piss flooding his boxers and running down his leg.

"Maybe a girl just needs to be left the fuck alone.

That ever occurred to you, Liam? That a woman is not your possession? I'm showing you what possession looks like. I'M TALKING TO YOU!" Eddie put his hands up, startled. "You never seemed like you got scared so easily CREEP. Is it because it's your son talking and you never thought he'd find out? You really thought you were going to get away with it?"

"Our Father in heaven...hallowed be thy name...thy kingdom come, thy will...be done..." "You think God is going to forgive you? For what you did?" "...On earth as it is in heaven..." "You think that if I cut you open with this blade, He's going to receive you with open arms? After what you've done? Seriously?"

"I'm..sorry..." "What?" "I'm sorry Jacinda!" "You're sorry? CREEP. Really?" "Yes!" "And this is how the story ends? The murderer has repented and the evil spirit disappears into the night...probably ascending into light because it is all over. How sweet. I CAN BE FREE!" "Yes! Yes, you're free. I never meant to hurt you!"

Jacinda looked around. "This is a really nice house. I like your car." She pointed across from her. "I've never seen a bed so big. Really nice." She proceeded to sit on the corner of the bed. "What a price to pay for your sins. All nice things. Hmm. Nice slippers. Bedsheets are nice. It's NICE. IT'S NICE! Bet you couldn't last a day alone in a watery grave. Hope no one splits your head in two." "What do you want from me?!"

"I want you to come with me." "What?" "You heard me. I want you to come with me. NOW!" Eddie stumbled out of bed and wiped his neck. He nervously put on his shoes. "No shoes!" Jacinda pointed the knife at Eddie and commanded him to walk down the steps. They got into Umezda's car and she told him to drive.

"I don't...know how all of this happened...with you possessing...my son and all, but I really, really regret killing you Jacinda. You have to believe it! Please!" "Keep driving." "I'm sorry!" Jacinda pressed the knife to his neck and said, "DRIVE."

When they got to the park, Jacinda pointed to the ground. "Dig." "Dig? I don't have a shovel." "DIG!" "Whaa..." "Are you deaf? I said, DIG!" Eddie got on his knees and dug his fingers into the dirt. Claw after claw until he drew blood from broken branch pieces. He dug until he collapsed over. "You don't get to die on my grave CREEP. Keep digging."

The sunrise illuminated the sullen park. Birds were chirping and Eddie was nodding off, bone-weary. He was slouching over, his lips cracked and purple. His fingertips were bloody and numb and his back aching. He finally brushed his worn fingers across bone. "KEEP DIGGING. Make sure all the bones are exposed." "I'm... so tired...so tired..." "There's no sleep for The Wicked. You should know that CREEP."

After Eddie exposed all of Jacinda's bones, he carried them to the car. "You're going to drive to the police station and I want you to tell them what you did to me and where the body was buried. And if you decide to drive this car off a bridge, just know...you'll be killing you AND your son. And I'll be waiting for you on the other side."

Drained and weak, Eddie forced his body onto the driver's seat and turned on the ignition. He pressed his forehead to the wheel and sobbed uncontrollably. "I bet you want mercy at this point, don't you? But you never gave me that courtesy. Oh, the sins of the Father. NOW DRIVE CREEP!" Jacinda said, pressing the knife to his side. As Eddie drove, he occasionally looked over to his side and saw glimmers of Jacinda's eyes and lips. "This was for the best Jacinda. If you kill me, I'm at peace with that. Just don't kill Umezda. He's a good kid. I beg of you." Jacinda pushed the knife slightly into Eddie's side and he screamed.

They arrived in front of the police station and Eddie pressed his hands against his side to stop the blood. "Now turn the car off and go inside." "I can't." "Sure you can CREEP." "I'm not a creep! I'm not that man I used to be Jacinda! Please! You have to get that through your skull!" "YOU BASHED IN MY SKULL! You don't get to act like a martyr! You never told anyone where my body was! Never! That's how much you cared! You were never sorry. You were guilty! Those are two different things Eddie."

"So what am I supposed to do Jacinda? Go in there, accept my fate and go to jail? I'm older now. I can't..." "You can't choose your fate anymore Eddie. No more being selfish. No more thinking that your sins can be erased. Because you don't really confess to them. If you really want to feel God...I mean REALLY feel His love...tell the police what you did."

Eddie lifted one tired leg after the other. In a dirty tank top and boxers, soaked in urine and sweat, he walked up the steps and into the police station. "Uh? Can I help you?" A woman called out from behind a glass. "Yeah. Uh, yeah...I wanna...I wanna report a crime." "A what?" "A Crime...I committed...34 years ago?"

"Okay. And what is that?" Two cops positioned their hands to their guns. "I murdered a 17 year-old..." Eddie took a deep breath and with tears streaming down his face, he said "JACINDA LUKAS."

"Get down on your knees!" Jacinda looked on as Eddie was being escorted into a car. She began to cry. She cried for the time she lost. Cried for her death. And she cried for her life.

"Thank you." She whispered. Umezda returned to his body and looked down at his hand. He noticed there was only some blood on the knife and he tossed it to the backseat. He looked up as his father passed him. He got out of his car. A cop approached him. "Hey, are you that guy's son?" "Yes." "Okay. We need to ask you some questions."

CHAPTER TWENTY:

HOMECOMING

Every year a spool of children enter this glorious place; their minds are full of wonder with occupying space. Who dares to know what one does think or how one should react; Umezda does this for you, my dear this is a fact. And while you enter splendor, receiving what is great, know everything afforded to you has a name and a face. Remember well your journey, remember well your claims; tomorrow could be one thing, the next could be your fate.

That lullaby had been passed down from generation to generation; particularly in The Lukas Family. Its origin was delicately seeped in brusks of European folklore. Dutch, Belgian and Swiss legends, likened to the stories of Sinterklaas and others meant to keep children from misbehaving. This resonated with Jacinda as a child and she enjoyed hearing about it every night.

Josie remembered bits and pieces of it too, and decided to look it up on the internet. She typed in several words and phrases but nothing came out. After a while, she gave up and called her youngest daughter Noelle. "Mom, are you even on Checkmate?" "Checkmate?" "Yeah, it's a search engine where things pop up easily. These other websites are too controlled by this government."

"Okay, well look it up for me. I'll wait." Noelle typed in "spool of children" and the story popped up. "You want me to send you a link or a screenshot?" "Ugh, no. I'll have to hang up and then check it and I'm not good with all of that. Just read it to me." "Read it to you? But mom, I'm in the middle of something."

"Come on! Stop being difficult and just read it." "God! Okay, hold on:

'Every year a spool of children enter this glorious place; their minds are full of wonder with occupying space. Who dares to know what one does think or how one should react; Umezda does this for you, my dear this is a fact. And while you enter splendor, receiving what is great, know everything afforded to you has a name and a face. Remember well your journey, remember well your claims; tomorrow could be one thing, the next could be your fate.

If dragons tried to harm you, if lizards came untamed; Umezda Great and Powerful would save you on this day! Oh, come now little children; gather round all sweet and gay. Though spirits often wander, they come back just to play. But if one among you changes, and the rest of you stay behind, we shall summon back, for all of us one kind.'

Is this supposed to be like some religious kid's book or some weird metaphysical stuff?" "I'm not too sure. It was something your grandmother would read to us at night, before we went to bed." "Creepy." "Well, it was a different time." "I love vintage." "Oh calm down!" Josie snapped. "If you want to hear about something creepy, I'll tell you what happened one night to your aunt Jacinda and I."

"Oh yay! Memory lane!" "You can pack up that sarcasm for your father. Do you wanna know or what?" "Of course! I was just joking mom." "Well, after we were told to go to bed, I would slip into Jacinda's bed and we would joke and talk and run our fingers up and down each other's backs. It would calm us as we giggled into the night.

One night, while we whispered and talked about what happened that day, something walked past our bedroom. I noticed it first and hid my face against Jacinda's chest. She looked up and noticed that whatever that thing was, it was making its way back. It was so strange; it looked like it had a sheet over its head and it stood directly across from us. It was so ominous it gave me goosebumps!

We were so frightened and we barely made a sound. All we could hear was heavy breathing. But it wasn't coming from us. Then just like that, it turned around and disappeared." "It was probably your mother and father playing tricks on you two. Parents always know when they're kids are up when they're not supposed to be, right?" "That's what we thought too. But the following night it returned.

It made its way past the door, then back eventually. It just…stared at us, breathing and then disappeared. On the third night, we decided to take a Polaroid picture of it. It came back around the same time and Jacinda had her camera under the sheets. When it decided to settle at the doorway, Jacinda pulled out the camera and quickly snapped a photo.

And just like that, it vanished, never coming back again. I pulled out a flashlight and when I pointed it at the photo, all we could see was something that resembled a little boy. That always stuck out to me in my mind. That resonates with me to this day because it always reminded me of that story." "So you equated the two. That's common in childhood fears and phobia. Is that photo in some paranormal museum or something, cuz' you guys literally filmed a ghost." Noelle smiled.

"I don't know what happened to that photo, but I'm sure if I go to mom's house, she'll have it in one of Jacinda's boxes." "Grandma still has aunt Jacinda's things, after all these years?" "She's held onto some things. We can go there and check it out if you'd like. Maybe sometime this weekend?" "I think that would be fun. If we find it, can we sell it on eBay?"

"IF you find it." Josie scrolled through photos on her phone and found some of her sister's tombstone. She couldn't believe that her sister's body was finally found. It was surreal because she had given up on the fact that it could ever happen. She was almost 49 and figured she would never see the day. But she did.

She still had Umezda's number but was weary about having a conversation with him after everything that happened. She just couldn't get it out of her head that the man who killed her sister was the father of her Medium. It was beyond words. She felt betrayed. She felt that this kid had lured her in to get information or something. But then she remembered that she reached out to him first and that maybe he didn't know what happened.

It was also an eerie coincidence that the lullaby she remembered from long ago, had the same name as the young Medium. "Maybe he knew that lullaby and took the name for himself." She thought. "That's definitely a possibility." Josie snagged a few peanut butter cookies from a box in her pantry, dropped them on a plate and then headed to her bedroom.

She returned to the living room to grab her cellphone. She scrolled through her numbers and saw a missed call. Umezda Wicker." She got in bed and turned on Golden Girls. She glared at her phone, fidgeting with it until she decided to call him back. "Yes, Hello....it's Josie from....the other day? I think we need to maybe have that talk. I need a lot of questions answered."

"I think that's a perfectly good idea. Because I have so much to tell you." "Okay, but remember that this is all new to me and I'm freaking out about...everything." "I understand. It's been quite the experience for me too! You might not fully believe what I'm going to tell you, but it's all true. It all happened for a reason." "Well, seeing how things turned out, I think it needs to be heard."

"I'm glad you called back. Would you like to come over for coffee tomorrow?" "Uh, maybe we should meet at a public place. For my safety?" "Sure! Sure, that sounds plausible." "Okay." "Alright." "Um, yeah." "Well, tomorrow? Carlen's Cafe? 2pm?" "Okay, sounds good. Thanks Umezda." "Thank you Josie."

Umezda walked into the cafe in a pair of black skinny jeans, a Kylie Minogue t-shirt and a gray jacket. He placed his laptop bag on one of the chairs and proceeded to order. "I'll just have the hazelnut latte, extra sweet please. Thank you. Oh! And I'll do the blueberry muffin. Yep, you can heat it up, thank you! That'll be it." Umezda sat down, rubbing his face and trying to make sense of it all.

He looked around, trying to see if she was nearby. He got antsy and started to rummage through his bag until the young man came over with his latte and blueberry muffin. "Thank you. Yes, place it right there! Thanks!" He pressed a piece of the muffin into his mouth and chewed it slowly. Josie walked in, she plopped her large purse on one of the other chairs and sat down.

"We'll have to make this quick, I have to run some errands." She sat across from Umezda with big sunglasses and a slick ponytail. She sat back leisurely, crossing her legs. "Do you want anything?" Umezda asked. "No, I'm not really hungry. I've just been biting off all my nails since last night and I just want to get this over with."

Umezda ogled at her fingernails and smirked.

"We can always do this another time if you're in such a rush Josie.
I totally get it." "I have time. Just not too much time." Umezda was
trying to hide his frustration and took another bite of his muffin.
"Okay, so..." "Yeah?" Umezda could feel the icy reception so he
shifted in his chair and sipped on his latte.

"Anyway, I brought my laptop. I thought I could show you what
happened. I was doing some writing last night, putting bits and pieces together and I really don't want to prattle around explanations.
So it's all there." "I don't need to see what's on the laptop. You're
doing just fine." "Oh? Um, okay. Sure." There was a dislodged silence between the two. Josie observed Umezda and everything he
was saying.

"I'm not quite sure why you're so mad at me..." "Well let me give
you a reminder Umezda! You dragged me into one of your fake seances. I give you all these details about my sister, and then suddenly
there's this big news about YOUR FATHER being her murderer?
Don't you find that all a bit odd and fucked up? Because it's been
keeping me up at night."

"I never dragged you into any fake seances!" Umezda tried to keep
his voice down. My seances are real. I do have a real gift. Or whatever you want to call it. But I definitely have it. That is not up for
discussion, with all due respect. I think that perhaps our meeting
was fate." "Really?" She said sarcastically. "Josie, you called me for
a reading. You told me you saw me on some local show and you
wanted a reading with me.

I told you I might be booked and you said you didn't mind reading
with a group." "So?" "So, my point IS that our meeting was not my
doing. And that day, you Leah and Anette were over, and we made

contact, but not with your sister. It was some other spirit named Blaire. You remember right?"

"Uh-huh, and?" Umezda sank back, rolling his eyes. He felt himself feeding off of the negative energy and he started to collect his things. "Where are you going?" "Clearly, you don't want to be here and I can't force you to be here. I'm not defending myself Josie! I didn't do anything wrong!"

"You are connected to the man who murdered my sister! YOU! You could have told me that when we met. You didn't have to hold back that information." "I didn't hold back any of that information. That's why we're here. So I can explain what happened. But you came in here defensive and angry and it's not going well, so maybe we can talk another time."

Josie grabbed Umezda's arm. "Wait." Umezda looked at her and sat back down. "Umezda this is really hard for me. I've been struggling for a long time. My family and I have been dealing with this since forever. My mother is not around to see this and so it's all been a whirlwind of emotions. I apologize if I offended you but it's really fucking hard. Like really hard."

"I get it. I do. Finding out your father isn't who he really is, is kind of a shocker too." "I saw that. He changed his identity. But what was the point in that? He didn't live very far from where it happened. He got away with it because that police department didn't care." "Right, but times have changed."

"Times never change. People remain the same Umezda. Cops don't suddenly care because there's a new chief in office. Or if there's some other people on the case. Things go missing, rape kits go untested, murders go cold and they stay cold." "I know all of that is true, but what happened here is beyond anything I can rationalize. I'm going to, but you might not believe all of it."

"Try me." "My father...his urge to dig up the bones...your sister's bones? What happened that night." Umezda lowered his voice. "It's not ideal to speak about all of this here, but it'll have to suffice." "I just wanted a neutral place. That's all." "I hear you. Well..." Umezda looked around.

"Your sister came to me. That night." "What?" "Your sister, she came to me that night." "I heard you! What do you mean?" "It was her. She did it. She made my father dig up her bones." "You're playing with me, right?" "Please Josie, hear me out. I'm coming from a sincere place. I really am. It was strange for me too."

"She possessed my body. It was something extraordinary ! And then she made me drive..." "Oh, I don't think I can hear this. This doesn't make sense!" "Will you hear me out?!" "I'm sorry. Yes. Go on." "She possessed my body! I cannot explain it. She had a lot of power. A lot of it. And I'm not too sure how it was possible but she did it. She forced me into my car. We drove to my father's house... and she forced him to dig up her bones."

"She did?" Josie's eyes welled up. "What did she look like?" "Well, she possessed my body so I can't really tell you. But it was a very terrifying experience. I didn't know what she was going to do at first. She pulled a knife from my butcher's block. That made me nervous. I thought she was going to kill him or kill me. I was freaking out. But she managed to get the job done. And everything that was revealed really left me in awe, but it also made a lot of sense. I'm a bit banged up from that night but it had to take place."

"Did...did she want to see me?" "I mentioned it. And her emotions were all over the place. I could feel the longing for it. It was cosmic and beyond supernatural. But she came to me for a reason. To get a proper burial." "She didn't want to be left out there alone. It's already been too long. Wow. Just..wow. How did it feel? To know that your father was a murderer?"

"I can't describe it. I wondered how many other women or people he murdered. I questioned my upbringing...his love. What he put my mother through before she died. It was some heavy stuff Josie. But I knew it wasn't just for me. I knew you wanted...not closure...I hate that word. Who wants closure when it comes to family?"

"I do. I've wanted it. I'm almost 50. I needed to know that she was okay. That even if she died...the way that she did...she was going to finally be at peace. I needed closure. But I know what you mean." "My father told me when I was a kid that my name came from a friend of his. Someone he cared deeply for. This is not a consolation or a glimmer of his innocence, but simply a reminder that he got my name from...Jacinda. Your sister." "How so?" "He said she dreamed up the name or something. That it was on some postcard. I'm not too sure..." "It was a lullaby. I was just reminded of it yesterday."

"A lullaby?" "Yes, something our mother would say to us. She held onto it I guess." "I find that to be special. That my connection to her is my name. Well, that's not the only thing connected to us. She's pretty strong." "Yeah she was...is." "I want you to know Josie that your sister didn't die in vain. And that she loves you very much. The love she has for you almost made my heart stop. If you ever wanted to make contact..."

"No, I think that I'm good Umezda. I want to see the trial play out. I want justice for my sister and I'm thankful that you helped make it all happen. I'm sorry that you had to find out the hard way that your father was who he is. But everything happens for a reason. If she really is out there, she'll find her way back to me."

Josie and Umezda embraced. Umezda kissed her cheek and said, "That same strength...that Jacinda had that night. All of that power...it's inside of you too. I can feel it." "You better believe it." After Josie left, Umezda sat there contemplating. He wondered if this was really his calling or if he should walk away from it all. Then he heard a voice. It wasn't a voice from anyone that was frequenting the cafe. The voice ran over with reverberation.

"Hello, I'm Clarissa."

CHAPTER TWENTY ONE:

ONE BY ONE

Geraldine laid naked on her backside, her breasts exposed. Phillip pressed his leg on hers and kissed her lips. "You were sensational tonight Mr. White!" Phillip made his way to Geraldine's nipple and licked it. "I could go for round two if you'd like?" Phillip remarked. "Hold your horses! I need to catch my breath!" "You're a tigress. I didn't know you tasted so good!"

"This might not be the right time to say this Phillip, but what about your wife?" "What about her?" "Well, is she okay? I mean...is she?" "She's fine darling. What I told you at the restaurant was small talk. I don't want you repeating my business around the town. That's social suicide." "Oh, no sir I would never! I just..."

"Shhh! You just what? Don't tell me you're a softy?" Geraldine jumped on top of Phillip and licked his lips. "I'm just making sure that when you get home, you don't have any problems. That's all." "Phillip was rock hard. He positioned himself to enter Geraldine but she got off of him.

"I thought you said she was loony? You said she was gonna go to some doctor soon? What's taking so long?" "Hey! What is that any of your business? Don't you like having fun?" "Of course I do! I just really like you!" "So then prove it to me." Geraldine began to ride Phillip. He pressed hard into her until he came.

"Gee, it's late! I should jump in the shower then head home. You can stay here if you like?" "No Phillip. I have a spouse too." "How's the ol' Gus?" "He's fine." "Oh, good! Fine young man that Gus." "Phillip?" "Yeah doll?" "I want to leave him." "Leave him?

Now why would you want to do that?" "I'm in love with you Phillip!" Phillip laughed, tossing her her panties. "You're infatuated is what you are. You like my big Johnson and my muscular body. That's why I work out Geraldine. Women like that." "Women? I thought we had something special?"

"Cut it out Geraldine, I'm married! Don't pretend like this is something it's not. I love my wife and I intend on keeping it that way. Besides, you can't be a wife to two men. Right? Come join me in the shower." Geraldine put on her undergarment and slipped on her skirt and blouse. She made her way out of the room and into the elevator.

She began to sob, dabbing her cheek with the back of her hand, wiping the tears. "You're such a sucker Geraldine Louise!" She said in the elevator reflection. She swiped at her head with her fist and pressed "Lobby." When the door opened, she made her way towards the front exit but a voice called out her name. "Geraldine?" "Yes?" Geraldine wiped her face and tucked her handbag under her arm.

"Can I help you?" The young woman gave Geraldine an unpleasant look. "Well?" She chimed, snapping her finger. "My name is Piper and I'd like a word with you." "I don't know you so..." "Sure you do!" Piper grabbed Geraldine's arm and strolled down the hallway. "Let go of me at once!" Geraldine snapped, trying to pluck away but Piper's fingernails dug into her arm, pulling her closer.

"Listen here you harlot!" "Why I've never!" "I'd like you to know that I am well aware of what you're doing with my friend's husband and I want you to stop it." "Stop it? I'm doing no such thing!" "I have photographs, Geraldine. Plenty of them. Too many, in fact. Why, they're all scattered across my kitchen table."

"Who are you again?" Piper pulled Geraldine closer. "Don't make such a spectacle. No one likes a sassy tart." "Unhand me this instant!" "Here's what's going to happen Geraldine..." Piper dug her nails deeper until she drew blood. You're going to stop seeing Phillip White and you're going to stop coming out of an elevator looking like a wet newspaper.

If you so dare ruin my friend's life with your gaucherie, I will not only send those photos to your husband Gus, but I will rip your eyes out! Maybe you'll contemplate your whore ways with some alone time in the dark."

"He doesn't love me! So maybe that won't be so hard." "He's taken. You do realize that, right? He made a vow. Not to you. Not to his company. To his wife. I know you've decided early on that you're a homewrecker, but maybe the real message for Gus is sending you home in a box. Maybe he likes puzzles and he can try to put you together again like Humpty Dumpty."

"You crazy woman! Is that a threat?!" "It's a promise." Geraldine noticed a ring on Piper's finger. "You're his wife! He said you were fucking nuts! Just demented! A lunatic!" Piper let go of Geraldine's arm and stepped away. She grew anxious as she watched Geraldine run away from her.

Piper felt unbalanced. Her hands started to tremble and she made her way to a seat. "You okay ma'am?" An attendant asked. "I'm fine, thank you!" Then suddenly, her head tilted back and her eyes went from green to brown. "Actually, maybe you can help me. There's a young woman wearing a brown mink fur making her way towards the front of the hotel building. Can you kindly tell her that a 'Mr. White' wants her to stay put?" "You mean the young lady with the yellow silk blouse?"

"Yes, Geraldine is her name." "Sure thing! And what's your name?" "Ruby." "Well then Miss Ruby, I'll do just that!" The attendant made his way across the hotel and out the front doors. Geraldine was waiting for her car to come around. "Miss? Are you Geraldine?" Ruby looked down at her nails and sighed. "Maybe not red for this occasion." Her hands began to change, her nail color going from red to pearl.

She tossed her jacket over her shoulder and made her way outside. "Thank you." She said to the attendant but he seemed confused. "I'm sorry, who are you?" "Hello, I'm Ruby." She grabbed Geraldine by the hair and yanked a chunk of it in her fist. "Maybe Piper wasn't clear." Geraldine let out a scream, sprawling her arms into the air in an exaggerated manner. Ruby punched her across the face and threw her against her car, as it arrived.

"She's ready to go home." Ruby yelled to the car attendant. She yanked Geraldine's brown mink fur coat and put it on. "Fits like a glove. I always go mad for mink." Geraldine drove off hysterical. Ruby walked to her car and got in. As they drove off, Piper felt sorry for Clarissa.

She yearned to look her in the face and tell her she needed to be strong. "Ruby, it's getting out of hand. You shouldn't have done that. She can go to jail for it. Or worse, the madhouse. Be more careful next time." "You're the one making threats. I simply came through to execute them." Piper turned, pulling into the driveway.

"Ruby, I've been doing some thinking, and maybe we should just put her out of her misery. What kind of life is it to be around only half the time? We've been sucking her dry. Maybe I could drive the car off a bridge somewhere. Maybe she'll be better off." "And what will happen to all of us?" Ruby interjected. "We just disappear into the unknown like before? I don't think so. She's not crazy because of us." "She's NOT crazy!"

"Well, I'm just saying! Clarissa has a lot of power and it'll take a lot more than driving off a cliff to finish her. Besides, that's a terrible idea. She needs us just as much as we need her. She's a saint. We could never achieve the things we have without her transcendent energy. That power is massive!"

"We can't decide that for her." Piper said. "It has to come out of her. And she doesn't want any of it." "We're not entirely sure that's true Piper. She's been playing the sweet little suburban housewife for a while now. Nothing out here is catered to her. Look at her douche bag husband, fucking anything that moves. Her mother is gone, she doesn't have much of a family. No one is looking out for her best interest but us."

"Jacinda was clear that after you girls were done, it was time to move on." "Fuck Jacinda. She's off being the heroine. She sucks up most of the energy anyway. She should be grateful." "She is grateful. We just can't play these games with Clarissa's life. None of you understand how I feel about this. I've been with her since the very beginning." Rachel couldn't believe what she was hearing. "None of you have a say in this. We are all dead. It sucks to be us but it's true! Clarissa, on the other hand is alive and well and here we are playing destiny and fate with her. She's stronger than you both know and I don't just mean telekinetically. She brought us out for a reason!"

"We're just saying that..." Ruby added, "We're all part of her heart lines now. You don't really care because they found your bones.

You've been buried in a Mausoleum. I don't see you going to the light." "It's not that simple. They haven't caught those assholes yet. And I'm not going anywhere until they do. And what are you going on about? You murdered an entire family in retribution." "They had it coming." "Oh, I'm sure!" Rachel said sarcastically.

"I just want to see my children." Blaire added. "And every time Clarissa is present, it doesn't happen. I miss them more than anything in the world and I can't reach them. Every time I'm close...she pulls them away." "We can't rely on her to fix all of our problems. We have to accept that she's doing as much as she can. She's one person. Even if it seems like she's more. She's only ONE." Rachel said.

"If I am able to see them and touch them, I can consider leaving. Lightening the load. But she's made it so difficult. Every time she says she feels better, I have to wait until she's not. That guy Umezda is the only person that seems to help us shift that energy. He's the only one that can help us. But he's not here yet. We have to constantly live in these multiverses, hoping it'll all connect again. It's exhausting back and forth. That's why she's so drained."

"What happens when we've all achieved what we want? We leave her alone? We just disappear? What will she do without us?" Piper asked. "She loves us just as much as we love her. Or maybe we're using her too much. We're sucking up so much of her energy that it's creating a block. Maybe we're the reason she's having so much power. If we leave, maybe it'll go away and she can live a normal life."

Clarissa awoke, putting her arm around her husband. His warm dewy skin was under a jumble of blankets, his muscular chest with swirls of hair protruding. She snuggled close to him and kissed his neck. "Make love to me." She whispered. "He slowly opened his eyes and swooped her into him. "What?" "Make love to me. Maybe we can make some babies?"

Phillip kicked off the blankets and skittered his fingers across her porcelain shoulders. "I would love to make love to you my sweet angel." Clarissa slipped her hands into his underwear and slowly pushed them down. She could feel his heat pulsating on her skin and she wanted more of it. "Uhhh..." He ran his fingers against his tongue and slowly rubbed until she moaned. Pleasuring her, he turned her around and lightly nibbled on her ear.

"I want you inside me!" She exclaimed, wet and writhing in ecstasy. He pulled her close and pushed deep inside. He went in and out as her head pressed against the pink silk pillows. "I want it! Give it to me! Yes!!" Phillip went faster like a jackhammer. He could feel he was getting close. He thrusted into her and as he did, he fell on top of her yelling "I'm gonna shoot!" Clarissa screamed, her eyes changed into ovals of white.

She shook with euphoria, each bedroom window shattering. Startled, Phillip fell off the bed. "What in the world?" He stumbled on the blankets, tangling his feet and hitting his head against the bureau. Clarissa began to violently convulse. Her mouth began to foam and her hair changed from color to color. Phillip watched in awe as she levitated towards the ceiling. "Clarissa! Clarissa please! Not again!" Clarissa turned her head towards Phillip and then fell back onto the bed.

"Clarissa?" He called out, walking slowly towards her. And then, in a deep and raspy guttural voice, she responded, "Clarissa? Clarissa doesn't live here anymore."

CHAPTER TWENTY TWO

THE DAMAGE IS DONE

"Mother, I'd like a glass of milk please." Jane fixed her gaze upon her daughter, eyes vast and anxious. She turned back to her guest, lifting a finger, muttering "Give me just a moment." She got up, dusting off her high waisted sailor pants. She lowered her head towards Clarissa's and said "I specifically told you it was bedtime. What does mommy say about drinking anything after 8?"

"That I should not get up except to use the lavatory." "Right! I'll make an exception this once." She lightly pinched Clarissa's nose and made her way towards the kitchen. She pulled out a jar of milk and poured some into the glass. "Be very careful! No messes. What does mother say about messes?" "Messes need not be unless it is intentional." Jane placed a hand on her hip and waited by the counter impatiently, drumming her manicure on the marble counter while her daughter finished every drop. She patted Clarissa on the head and pointed her towards the back steps.

"To sleep with the angels my dear." With a clenched jaw, Jane made her way back into the parlor and flung her arms in the air. "She's gone. My apologies! Do continue where you left off." Greta nibbled on a piece of fruit with skepticism and then lightly wiped the juice from her thin lips. "I won't keep you and I won't beat around the bush Mrs. Adelberg. Your child is infected." "Infected? Come again?" "She's with Abyzou."

Jane was mortified, tapping her foot nervously. "That is impossible! We are good Jews. That does not exist here and you are sadly mistaken!" Jane stretched her fingers in a dismissive way. "Clearly this was a mistake. Good day, I say to you Mrs. Todalov." Greta shrugged her shoulders and placed her hands on her knees.

"If you are fine and in favor of the changeling living inside your home, that is up to you. I'm here because you rang me, though it is a great disturbance to take me from my home to yours at this time of night only to toss me to the street. It is poor etiquette. And you say 'good Jews!'"

"Pardon my chagrin Mrs. Todalov, but when you say my child is a changeling AND may be possessed by the devil, well..." "I am here because you have something evil that lurks beneath. I am here to help you and your household resolve this issue within her. If you do not wish for my services, I am happy to leave. I'll become a burden no longer."

"Abyzou?" Jane whispered. She raised her eyebrows in disdain and motioned for Greta to sit. "I was hoping to hear something different. Perhaps...childish fits. Children have fits, correct?" "Under normal circumstances Mrs. Adelberg, The Abyzou does not fully possess any one person or child. It is rare in this age for her appearance to be so strong. It is possible that your daughter, if she is not a changeling...could be completely under the influence of this demon."

Greta hastily opened her bag and pulled out a necklace. "She must wear this amulet and it must have the fingerprints of both you and your husband along with the child's. She must never take it off, even when she bathes until she is a woman. It will serve as a protection. I do not suggest an exorcism. Catholicism does not possess the power to take out any demons except The Blood of The Lamb." "The Blood of The..." "The Blood of The Lamb, that's right."

Jane took hold of the amulet and kissed it. "Thank you Mrs. Todalov. Thank you! Is that it? Do you need to bless her room? Bless the child?" "No. God is with her. God will protect her. She is innocent. Abyzou is a polluted beast and when she is of age, that beast will find its way back to the darkness."

"How, may I ask, did she become possessed with it in the first place?" "Clarissa is an object of her envy. She desires to be like Clarissa but she cannot. One day your child will give birth to many daughters and those daughters will also be the envy of Abyzou."

"Why did she choose my child?" "Your child is simply a pathway. A strong and in fine fettle. Her innocence and blood is pure and so this demon wants to contaminate that. For many centuries it has tried to pollute bloodlines but has failed. Is there something in your daughter's life that has caused her great grief?"

Jane covered her mouth. "Her father! He went off to war and we've been so anxious to hear from him. It's affected Clarissa in a most profound way. Her pain is so severe. She has night terrors of her father beheaded, coming home in a casket. Oh, it's simply awful! Could that be it?"

"It is quite possible, but not enough to summon the attention of something so foul. You must think Mrs. Adelberg. What is afflicting your babe, that it has pulled her in completely?" Jane scratching her forehead, walked around the room. "This is all so staggering, I can barely think!" Greta walked towards Jane and dug her nails into

Jane's palms.

"If you are lying to me, you are lying to yourself Mrs. Adelberg. That beautiful young girl is your child and whatever happens to her, you will never forgive yourself." Jane pulled away and rubbed her hands. "I don't lie, how dare you? I'm just distraught. Don't you see this makes me fearful for her safety?"

Jane placed the amulet in her pocket and sat down. "So? What now?" Greta glared at Jane with suspicion and pulled out a box of cards. She placed seven cards on the table upside down. "What's this?" Jane quipped. "This will help reveal the truth." "No more of this for tonight. I'm consumed with fright. I won't be able to sleep!"

Greta ignored her and flipped the first card over. "This speaks of a group. It could be a family or a group of friends. There is something going through it, which means that something is not right." Jane shifted in her chair and crossed her arms. Greta flipped the other card. "The dead are asleep." "I beg your pardon?" "I said the dead are asleep. There is interference."

Greta snickered, looking around the room and flipping the third card. "Women." "Women?" "Many women from many lives are coming through. They are with your daughter." "My mother, I suppose. My grandmother. My sister passed away from tuberculosis. Maybe she is there as well?"

Greta tossed the fourth card on her lap. "Dimensions. Spirit realms. The here and the after. Mrs. Adelberg, are you sitting in the middle of something?" Jane's eyes widened and she looked under her chair. "Don't be rude. I am revealing what you need to hear and see."

Greta turned the fifth card over. "Redemption of the soul. Something will be redeemed. Anything uniformly negative will not prosper." Jane reached over and turned the sixth card nervously. "Well? What does that say?" "You're a liar. That you have been keeping something from your child. What might that be?"

Jane grew nervous and rammed a piece of fruit into her mouth. "Silly. This all sounds silly!" She mumbled. Greta rolled her eyes and flipped over the seventh card. She picked up all seven cards, placing them back in the box, and then into the bag. She walked over to Jane and placed her hand out."

"What?" She asked, consumed with guilt. "Give me the amulet! I wasted my time. I shall be on my way." Jane, flustered, pulled the amulet out but kept it bundled, in her fist. "What did that card say Mrs. Todalov?" Greta wrestled the amulet out of Jane and struck her across the face. Shocked, Jane struck her back.

"Why I...I...never...why would you dare?" Jane cried, running to the door. Greta placed the amulet in the bag and pointed at Jane. "You are evil incarnate! Obidchick rebenka! What you have done to your daughter, to curse her with such things! It is wicked!" Jane grabbed Mrs. Todalov by the arm and shoved her out, slamming the door behind her.

Jane tried to maintain her composure but she was overwhelmed with dread. She slammed her fists against the door and slid to her knees. She wiped her tears and got up. She made her way to the kitchen and into the linen closet. She pushed away candles and table covering to reveal a silver blade hidden away from sight. Apprehensive, she pressed the blade to her chest and took a deep breath. "She has to understand." She went up the stairs and down the hall. She walked into her daughter's room and stood over her.

She lifted the blade, shaking uncontrollably; determined to finish what she started. "I'm so sorry my little princess!" Sobbing, she plunged the blade into her daughter's chest. She pulled the knife out and stabbed her again and again. She began to scream, falling over her daughter, running her fingers through her blonde hair. "Oh my sweet beautiful baby! I'm so sorry! Forgive me! Oh, Clarissa please forgive me!"

Clarissa spit out blood and reached for her mother's hand. Jane lifted the knife. And when she went to stab her again, Clarissa's hands rose. "Mother!" She cried out. Jane flew across the room. She fell over, breaking her arm. She tried to get up, but Clarissa was sitting on the bed, her eyes glowing an ultraviolet.

"Darling, I'm sorry!" Jane screamed, but Clarissa didn't stop. She flicked her wrist and tossed Jane into the hall. Jane got up, holding her broken arm, trying to run down the steps. Clarissa stopped Jane, flinging her into the air. "Mother but...I love you." "I...I love you too baby!" Jane cried. "Put mother down! Go on darling, put mother down! CLARISSA!"

Clarissa touched her chest, noticing that her hands were full of blood. "Mother, why would you want to hurt me? I thought you were different." "I...am...I am different darling! Please put mother down!" Jane screamed in horror.

"But you're not, mother. You're just like them. You're just like all of them!" Clarissa began to cry, coughing up blood. "I don't know how to fix it darling! I'm simply a wretched soul. I didn't know!" "You did know...you watched them do it to me mother!"

"Please Clarissa!" Jane pleaded. "I didn't know it would go this far! I...I tried to fix it! Please put mother down!" Jane could feel the bones in her legs cracking. She let out a primal yowl as her fingers snapped back one by one. "CLARISSA!" She screamed. "Mother did you ever love me?" The tears streamed down Jane's face. She could feel her stomach twisting, blood seeping from her eyes and ears. "C...la...riss...a.."

Clarissa pressed her bloody fingers to her lips and said "DIE." Jane snapped back, her body in flames. The screams echoed throughout the house. Jane's body fell to the floor, she gasped for air. "I said DIE." Jane choked on her own tongue, her eyes burning, bones piercing and protruding through her skin. Jane was dead.

Clarissa made her way down the steps, stumbling, holding her chest. She cried out as she slumped over at the bottom of the steps. When she awoke, she was at the hospital. The room was poorly lit, cold and silent. There was someone sitting across from her reading a magazine. "Hello?" She called out, but the person just strummed her fingers throughout, turning each page. "Are you my nurse?" The person looked up and was revealed to be a young woman. "How old are you?" She asked in a familiar voice. Clarissa slowly pulled herself up but the pain was intense. "Six ma'am." She managed.

"How sweet you are. Don't overexert yourself. Save the energy." "Where's my mother?" Clarissa asked. The young woman placed the magazine on the table and leaned forward. "I'm Piper. Just so you know." "Piper?" "That's right. I'll be taking care of you from now on." "But my mother..." "Nevermind her for now Clarissa. You're safe and sound. No one is going to hurt you anymore."

CHAPTER TWENTY THREE:

TRANSGRESSION

Taylor placed her summer read on the beach towel, taking in the salty sea air, and watching her seven year-old son who was making small sand castles a few feet away. It wasn't a particularly sunny afternoon, but she didn't mind as long as she was with her family. Her husband finally had some time off, and now was a better time than ever to be at The Hamptons.

"Hey!" She yelled to her daughter. "Go with your brother. He wants to get in the water." Her daughter nodded and took his hand in hers. Her cell phone began to ring and she rummaged through her beach bag for it. "Hey babe! Did you get the arugula?" "Yeah! I got some shrimp too!" "Mmm, that sounds delicious. I think Maddie and Tom are coming later tonight so get plenty!" "Got it!" "Thanks babe. Love you!" "Love you too!"

When Taylor put away her phone, a woman placed a collapsible chair next to her and said, "Hey! Is it okay if I park it next to you?" Taylor shrugged uncomfortably. "Yeah sure!" The woman sunk into the chair and put her hand out towards Taylor. "I'm Rosalind. And your name is?" Taylor was startled. She wasn't used to small talk but she entertained it. "Hi, I'm Taylor! Nice to meet you!"

Rosalind smiled and pointed to the little boy and girl playing near the water. "Are those your kids?" Taylor lowered her sunglasses.

"Mmhmm." "They're beautiful. The girl looks just like you. Come to think of it, they both do! You have strong genes!" "Ha! Well you should see their father." "The girl has your green eyes for sure. How sweet. They're so wonderful at that age." "What about you? Do you have children?" "Yes, I do!" Rosalind went into her pocket and pulled out a picture, handing it to Taylor.

Taylor took the photo in her hand. "Awe! Too cute! Two boys and a girl?" "That's right!" "I have two boys and a girl as well. Well, he's much older than them. He's my husband's son from a previous marriage." "It doesn't matter. Kids are kids, right?" "That's right! Are you from around here?" Taylor asked inquisitively. "Just here for the afternoon. You?" "We're on vacation. But just so you know, this is a private beach. See that house up there? That's connected to all of this."

"A beach connected to a house? That's fancy. You're all so lucky." Taylor pressed her sunglasses to her face, rolling her eyes. She laid back quietly, hoping the woman would leave. "My son is a singer." "Oh?" Taylor quipped. "Yeah, he's made quite the name for himself. I'm so proud of him." "Well that's awesome! Good for him!" "Yeah, good for him." Rosalind repeated.

"Do you bake with your kids?" "Excuse me?" "I said, do you bake with your kids?" "Oh, uh, sure. Karolina likes to make rainbow cupcakes and walnut brownies. She's actually good. It's scary!" Rosalind laughed. "That's sweet. My daughter is quite good with cupcakes too. She makes beautiful designs, uses all sorts of sprinkles and unique flavors. Ever have red velvet cake?"

"I have." "Mmm. She was so talented." "Oh? Did she pass?" "Sadly, yes." "Oh! That's terrible! I'm so sorry for your loss." Taylor plopped up and put her arm on Rosalind's shoulder. "I appreciate that. I really do!" "And you said your son is a singer?" "Yes." "Anything I know?" "I'm not too sure. Probably not your genre." "Well try me. I listen to all types of things and I'm dying to download some new music. Right now the kids and I are into Jazz."

"Miles Davis?" "I'm sorry?" "Miles Davis." "Oh! Is that your son's name?" Taylor pulled out her phone, looking up the name. "Miles Davis is a famous Jazz trumpeter. You said you were into jazz so I figured you knew who that was. Do you know Carmen McRae?" "No, I don't think so." "My mother would play her music when we were little. She had the voice of an angel." "Awe, that's so cute. I'll write those names in my notes. The kids would probably love it."

"I'm glad. Where's your husband?" Taylor didn't like personal questions from strangers. She began to gather her things and got up. "Children, we're going!" She waved and then looked down at Rosalind. "Well Rosalind, it was a pleasure but I really have to get dinner going." "Of course!" "Um...there's a public beach, I think... down a few blocks. Maybe you can go there? No rush!"

"I think I'll sit here for a few more minutes and then head off. Taylor, you have a beautiful family. Thank you for taking the time to talk to me. We'll talk soon!" "Yep!" Karolina and Ethan walked tentatively behind their mother as she rushed up the dunes and into the beach house. "Go to your rooms, showers then change!" They both nodded, heavy footed up the steps.

Taylor opened a bottle of Chenin Blanc and poured herself a glass. She sat at the island and opened up her laptop. She typed in "Carmen McRae" on iTunes and listened to Something To Live For. "Wow, she wasn't kidding." Henry opened the front door, fumbling with grocery bags. "Can the kids help?" "They're upstairs taking showers. Do you need my help?"

"Lemme see, no, I think I'm good. It's just one more bag." "I'll go get it!" "Okay!" Taylor kissed Henry and made her way to the car. While grabbing the last bag, she noticed Rosalind was standing across the street. She looked intently, making sure it was her. She waved and Rosalind waved back. "Do you need my husband to drive you to the beach or..." Rosalind smiled but didn't respond.

"Who are you talking to?" Henry asked, grabbing the bag from Taylor. "Some lady I just met. She's right over there." "Where? The Warners?" "No, she was standing over there. She must've left. It's fine. Just some lady I met at the beach." "Oh! That's cool!" "Yeah."

Taylor started on dinner while the kids sat quietly on their iPads in the family room. "Dinner's almost ready kids!" She yelled out. In unison, they put a thumbs up. "Henry, do you see your kids? Quiet! As usual! But wait til' the guests arrive. Then they can't keep their mouths shut." Henry ignored Taylor, scrolling through his phone.

When Maddie and Tom arrived, Ethan opened the door, waved then walked away. "So cute!" Maddie exclaimed. "The house looks gorgeous! My goodness you have the touch girl!" Taylor greeted them and walked them to the table. "Please eat! We have plenty! I have white and red...Chenin Blanc and Prosecco. I think we have Merlot out. Yes we do!"

"I'll have whatever you're having Taylor. You have a gorgeous tan!" "Oh my God, right? I don't know how, there was virtually no sun out since we got here." Henry shook Tom's hand and handed him a beer. "Tommy, where's your brother? Did he decide to stay in Jersey?" "Yeah, his wife hates The Hamptons." "I don't blame her!" They laughed and drank.

While they ate, Taylor placed a book in front of Maddie. "I am in love with this book! You won't believe what happens! Love!" Maddie flipped it and skimmed the back. "When you're done, I wanna read it." "Absolutely." Karolina tugged at her mom and pressed her face to her leg. "What's wrong honey?" "That lady is standing outside on the beach." "Huh? What woman, sweety?"

"That...woman. She's outside." "Just ignore her honey, people pass this place all the time!" Henry walked over to Karolina and got on one knee. "What woman honey?" "The woman mommy met earlier." Taylor's eyes grew. She walked across the family room and out to the deck. She scanned the beach to see if she saw anybody but nothing. She walked back inside and put her arm around Karolina.

"Honey there's nobody..." Suddenly, the lights went out. "Taylor where are the candles?" Henry asked. "Um, I dunno. We've never had to use them! Um...they might be upstairs." "Upstairs? Jesus!" The kids began to worry, taking out their phones as flashlights. Maddie laughed. "Shit happens Tay." Taylor turned on her phone flashlight and shined it at Tom.

"Damn that's bright! Are we going to tell ghost stories?" Taylor laughed. "Why is it that every time lights go out anywhere, we have to talk about ghosts?" Tom moved next to Taylor and put his hand on her ass. Taylor brushed off his hand and sat next to Maddie. "So, I think the kids are spooked because they think they saw some lady I met this afternoon on the beach." "Isn't it a private beach?" "Has that ever stopped anyone?" "True!" "She seemed nice. I dunno." Henry made his way downstairs with two lit candles and some other candles under his armpits.

Taylor helped him light the candles. "Babe, maybe you should go to the garage and check the fuse box and see if you can get the lights back on. There's not a storm or anything. And this never happens. Hope you paid the light bill." "Ha Ha, very funny! C'mon Tom!" Henry motioned. Maddie walked over to Taylor and said, "How's he dealing with everything?" "What do you mean?" "You know, the..."

Maddie pointed toward the kids.

"Oh! He's fine. He's trying to figure it all out with his attorneys, but I'm sure it'll be fine. I mean...he was doing his job, right?" "Yeah! Totally!" "I mean, there are times when he becomes antisocial and I let him. I know it's rough because he feels like a criminal even though he's not. You know?" "Yeah..." "He was just following orders and shit happens so, I'm always gonna stand by him. He needs to know he's not alone." "That's so great Tay. You're such a good person."

"Absolutely. We're not gonna fall apart because of some people rallying as usual. It's always the same shit. It's exhausting. Like, if you were not in the wrong place at the wrong time, like, I don't know what to tell you. Oh! There's peach cobbler for dessert! I know you love that!" "Yummy!" "Gimme just a sec...Karolina? Ethan? I want you where I can see you. No going outside. You hear me?"

Ethan tapped Taylor's arm, startling her. "Mommy, she went outside." "Who?" "Karolina." "She did? Wasn't she sitting down a minute ago? God! Gimme a minute Maddie, this is everyday." Taylor walked out to the deck and peaked her head out but she didn't see Karolina. She walked back inside and then towards the garage. "Henry, is Karolina with you?"

"Nope! We're just trying to figure out what happened here babe." "Okay!" Taylor ran back inside to where Maddie and Ethan were. "Did you guys see Karolina? Ethan, is she upstairs?" Ethan shrugged. "GO CHECK!" Ethan ran up the steps and went into Karolina's room but she wasn't there. He checked his room and then his parent's room, but nothing.

Taylor and Maddie looked for her in the front of the house but she was nowhere to be found. "Ethan!" She yelled. Ethan came running down the steps, gesturing that she wasn't up there. "Henry!" Taylor yelled. Henry stormed into the room and Tom followed. "It's Karolina! She's gone!" "What? How? Weren't you guys watching her? We were only gone a minute!" "I don't know!"

Taylor frantically knocked on neighbor's doors asking if they'd seen Karolina but everyone said they didn't. She went back into her house, scowering the place but Karolina was nowhere to be found. When the police arrived, Taylor was sobbing in the dark, holding Ethan in her arms. "I...I don't know what happened!" The officer asked if it were possible that Karolina went into the water, but Taylor shook her head no.

"We were eating and talking and she was fine! I...I don't know what happened! She was scared! She said she saw the lady from earlier this afternoon! I should've listened to her! Oh my God! Did she take my baby?!" Maddie placed a blanket over Taylor but Taylor pushed it off. "Go look for my child!" She scolded.

"We're going to do everything in our power to make sure we find your daughter Mrs. Lagialetta. We just need a picture." "A picture?" Taylor rummaged through her drawers and pulled out a picture of Karolina. "This was a few years ago! Most of my photos are on my phone. I..I can print them out at a Walmart..." "Sure. When you get them, give us a call. We'll go with this for now."

Taylor fell into Henry's arms. "How could this happen? How can they just take my child like that? This is supposed to be a safe area!" Henry kissed her head. "Calm down babe. We're gonna find her, okay?" Taylor looked up at him angrily. "This is your fault!" "My fault? What?" "Those fucking protesters! They took my kid! Because of you! You provoked them and now my child is gone! All because you killed that girl. Henry!!" Taylor had a nervous breakdown. She started to lash out at Henry, kicking and punching him. "Because of you, murderer! They took my baby!" Taylor's cry echoed throughout the beach house and outside.

A week later, Henry Lagialetta was charged for the murder of Tamika Sumley. Karolina Lagialetta was never found.

Made in the USA
Monee, IL
23 October 2020